Other *Matthew Martin* Books by Paula Danziger

EVERYONE ELSE'S PARENTS SAID YES
MAKE LIKE A TREE AND LEAVE
NOT FOR A BILLION GAZILLION DOLLARS

PAULA DANZIGER

EARTH TO MATTHEW

EARTH EARTH

PAPERSTAR

The Putnam & Grosset Group

TO SAMUEL ANTHONY DANZIGER,
Terrific Nephew and a great Consultant

Copyright © 1991 by Paula Danziger
Map courtesy of the Franklin Institute Science Museum,
Philadelphia, PA. All rights reserved. This book, or parts thereof,
may not be reproduced in any form without permission
in writing from the publisher. A PaperStar Book,
published in 1998 by Penguin Putnam Books for Young Readers,
345 Hudson Street, New York, NY 10014. PaperStar is a
registered trademark of The Putnam Berkley Group, Inc.
The PaperStar logo is a trademark of The Putnam Berkley Group, Inc.
Originally published in 1991 by Delacorte Press.
Published simultaneously in Canada.
Printed in the United States of America.

Library of Congress Cataloging-in-Publication Data
Danziger, Paula,
Earth to Matthew / by Paula Danziger. p. cm.
Summary: Matthew Martin finds himself on the threshold
of becoming a teenager in suburban America and experiences
conflicting emotions regarding his future. I. Title.
PZ7.D2394Ear 1991 [Fic]—dc20 91-4640 CIP AC
ISBN 0-698-11692-5
10 9 8 7 6 5

Acknowledgments

To Pam Swallow and Sue Haven—for listening daily, over the phone, to the manuscript

To Ann M. Martin, Martin, Martin for the echo-system, system, system

To everyone at The Franklin Institute, especially Marty Hoban and Elaine Wilner, and to the fantastic staff and volunteers who make Camp-In a wonderful, wonderful program

Chapter 1

"Ready for blast-off?" Mr. Martin turns to his son, who is sitting next to him in the car, eating a slice of pizza.

Matthew nods, pizza sauce dripping down his chin.

Mr. Martin pays the carwash attendant and pushes the button that rolls up the car window.

Matthew pretends to be the copilot. "Car in neutral."

"Check." Mr. Martin moves the stick shift to *N*.

"Foot off the brake," Matthew continues.

1

"Check."

"Pizza in mouth." Matthew hands his father a slice.

"Check." Mr. Martin folds the piece and starts eating it.

Outside, the attendant is hosing down the car and putting soap on it.

It's a family tradition at the Martin household. Every Saturday morning Matthew and his father take the sports car or the station wagon to be cleaned. Boy-Bonding Time is what Mr. Martin calls it.

Yuckoid is what Matthew's thirteen-year-old sister, Amanda, calls it.

"I don't want to Girl-Bond anymore. I prefer to think of myself as an only-child orphan," is what Amanda says.

Mr. Martin has made Matthew promise that in two more years, when Matthew becomes a teenager, he will not rebel . . . at least not against Boy-Bonding Time. Matthew's made the same deal with his mother for Matthew-Mom Bonding.

Sometimes Matthew thinks his parents are more like kids than the sixth-graders in his class.

The hosing ends and the car moves forward.

Brushes move against the side of the car.

"That tickles." Matthew jokes and laughs, even though he has made that statement every time the car has been washed since the tradition began five years ago.

"Martian asteroid monsters attacking overhead,"

Mr. Martin yells as the huge rubber strips go over the top of the car.

Matthew makes a sound like a machine gun and points the pizza slice at the strips.

As the car slides forward, leaving the strips behind, Mr. Martin breathes a make-believe sigh of relief. "Good work, partner. You've saved us once again."

A white light flashes, signaling that the underside of the car is getting washed.

Then the car gets polished and waxed and rust inhibitor is put on.

"Trouble up ahead," Matthew yells as something looking like a pool raft approaches the car.

"Duck," yells Mr. Martin as the machine blows the car dry. "Otherwise it's going to capture us and take us to its planet for scientific study. You have been chosen because they are planning special experiments to discover what causes some earthlings to have red hair and freckles. I will be kidnapped to act as their lawyer at intergalactic court if they ever get caught and put on trial for their dastardly deeds. I will refuse to defend them, of course, and they will send me into hyperspace, never to see my family again . . . never to eat your mother's tofu tuna casserole. Not eating the casserole is the good news. The bad news"—Mr. Martin ducks, pretending to avoid the machine—"is that never seeing my family again would be truly terrible, and I can't imagine Martian food. That just might be even worse than tofu and sprouts."

Matthew ducks. The car moves out of the building,

the attendants give it a final drying off, and the men of the Martin family stop ducking.

"Another successful mission. . . . We're back from outer space and the NASA technicians are cleaning off the radiation particles." Matthew sips his soda. "Once that is done, you can put the car antenna back up so that we can hear the latest earth music, the kind I like, not the old-fashioned junk that you listen to."

Mr. Martin acts upset. "How dare you call those masterpieces of music junk? Those, young man, are 'oldies but goldies.' "

" 'Oldies but moldies' is more like it." Matthew grins.

As they drive off, Matthew says, "Next week let's pretend we're surfers who wipe out and are rescued by a submarine that immediately has to go under the ocean."

Mr. Martin nods. "And now, young man, let's meet the rest of our family at the school. It's almost time for the big event . . . the dedication of the brand-new playground."

Matthew helped build the giant wooden-horse slide. He looks down at his thumb, which is still black and blue from missing the metal nail with the hammer and hitting the Matthew Martin one instead, and decides that the pain was worth it.

He thinks about how much fun the dedication is going to be, a real party with all of his friends there and lots of candy, cake, and soda.

Matthew hopes that his mother has not gotten all dressed up for this occasion. Lots of mothers get

4

dressed up, but not many mothers own a company that hires people to dress up in costumes to deliver messages. When Matthew's mother dresses up, it doesn't always mean a dress and heels. It sometimes means she puts on a gorilla or chicken suit or something like that.

The radio comes on.

"Now this is music." Mr. Martin grins and begins to sing along.

Matthew makes puking sounds in time to the music.

Mr. Martin takes the hint and turns off the radio.

Matthew stops making noises.

"Would you mind telling me what all the noise was about this morning?" Mr. Martin glances over at his son. "What were you and your sister fighting about? Why did you have to act like an alarm clock on one of the few mornings that your mother and I could sleep late?"

"It wasn't my fault." Matthew pretends that he is in a courtroom and that his father, the lawyer, is questioning him. "I'm innocent until proven guilty, and even then, I'm innocent."

"This isn't a court of law." Mr. Martin shakes his head. "I asked a simple question. I want a simple answer."

Raising his right hand, Matthew vows, "I promise to tell the truth, the whole truth, and nothing but the truth. I was in the vicinity of the kitchen on the morning in question and had just poured milk on my breakfast cereal and was in the process of putting bananas on top."

Mr. Martin tries not to grin. "Get to the point or I'm going to hold you in contempt of . . ."

He's not sure of what to hold him in contempt—court, car, parenthood?

Matthew continues. "The suspect entered the room."

"Are you referring to your sister?"

Matthew nods. "I said a simple hello and she yelled, 'Drop dead. You left the toilet seat up again.' In simple self-defense I had to throw the banana peel at her. No court in this country would convict me for doing that. If I get punished, I'm going to have to a-peel it."

Matthew laughs at his own pun.

So does Mr. Martin, who is trying not to.

"I rest my case," Matthew says.

"You may rest your case, but the noise kept your mother and me from resting ourselves . . . and the way you and your sister act sometimes is a clear case of a-rested development." Mr. Martin laughs at his own pun.

Matthew doesn't get it but laughs anyway so that his father stays in a good mood.

"In any case," Mr. Martin says, "if your sister shows up at the dedication, I want you to pretend that you like each other and stop this constant bickering."

Matthew protests. "She's the one who always starts it and now she's getting even worse. She doesn't even have to start, because she never stops. No matter what I do, she picks on me . . . and not just on me, on everyone. She yelled at Joshua the other day and he's not even her brother. He's my friend. And she and Mom are always fighting."

His father sighs. "I know."

"Why couldn't you have waited and just had me?" Matthew slurps some soda and then gargles it.

"Matthew . . . we love you . . . and we love your sister. I don't want you to think we don't. And you are not perfect either. Just remember all the times you have done things that were less than perfect. You're no angel either."

Matthew decides to pretend that he's on the witness stand again. "I *object.* No fair badgering the witness. I've done nothing wrong. She has . . . and you're picking on me."

Mr. Martin calls out, "Order in the court. Order in the court."

"I'll have two more slices of pizza and another can of soda and a couple of Mallomars and eleven Strawberry Twizzlers," Matthew says.

"What are you talking about?" Mr. Martin looks over at his son.

"You said, 'Order in the court,' so I'm ordering."

Shaking his head, Mr. Martin laughs. "Look, let's have a great time. This is a special day with a lot to celebrate. A new playground built on land that we managed to save for the town . . . Mrs. Nichols can not only stay on that land but the playground is being named for her."

Matthew nods and decides not to worry about

anything. So what if his sister exists? So what if his mother may be there dressed as a chicken?

His friends will be there.

So will a lot of junk food.

Nothing's going to ruin the fun.

Chapter 2

"Over the teeth and over the gums, look out, stomach, here it comes." Matthew wolfs down his fourth cupcake and takes a swig of his soda.

There's marshmallow icing across his upper lip.

Joshua Jackson, his best friend, reaches for a handful of chocolate chip cookies. "I can't believe that you aren't eating more of these. Mrs. Nichols made them. You know they are the best, the absolute best. I can't believe that you aren't eating these."

Holding open his backpack, Matthew shows that he has taken about a dozen of them.

Mrs. Martin approaches her son.

Matthew quickly zips shut his backpack.

His mother gets closer.

Matthew hopes that she doesn't notice how close he is to the junk food table. He also hopes that none of his friends realize that it is his mother, since she is dressed as a guinea pig.

Matthew hates having a parent who looks like a hairball and wishes that she had dressed like everyone else instead of getting into a costume to hand out helium balloons to all the little kids.

Standing directly in front of her son, Mrs. Martin points at him with one of her paws. "Young man, are you eating a lot of sugar? You know how I feel about that."

Shaking his head no, Matthew hopes that she doesn't do a breath check and then check his backpack, his pockets, and underneath the hat on his head.

She looks at his upper lip covered with marshmallow frosting, licks her paw, and reaches out to wipe off the marshmallow.

"Mom." Matthew backs off. "That's gross."

His father, who had changed into a guinea pig costume when he got to the playground, comes up and says, "It could be worse. Rodent moms lick faces."

"Gross." Matthew and his mother say at the same time.

Mr. Martin reaches for a doughnut.

Mrs. Martin takes it out of her husband's hand, puts it back on the table, and removes the can of soda from her son's grasp.

"I just want my family to be healthy. Please, honey, no more soda. There's fruit juice too."

Matthew wipes off some of the fur from the costume that has mixed with the marshmallow on his face. "Mom."

"Don't 'Mom' me," she says.

Matthew looks at his mother. "Guinea pig."

"Don't 'guinea pig' me either." She laughs.

A little boy interrupts, tugging at her leg. "Can I have a balloon?"

The little boy's mother says, "Did I hear a please?"

Matthew thinks of all the times his own mother has said that to him. He is willing to bet that the little kid's mother also uses her own spit to wipe off the kid's messy face.

Mrs. Martin hands the boy a balloon, pats him on the head, and turns back to Matthew. "Just remember, the dedication will begin in a few minutes. Why don't you stop eating and congratulate Mrs. Nichols for having the park named after her?"

"All right, Mom." Matthew picks up his soda again, sips it, and then gargles.

Mr. Martin says, "Look, there are a whole bunch of kids who haven't gotten balloons yet. Honey, why don't you go over to the ones by the equipment and I'll go over to the other side."

"Okay. See you later." She takes Matthew's soda out of his hand, empties it this time, and puts it in the correct garbage can.

After she leaves, Mr. Martin leans over to his son,

11

wiggles his whiskers, and whispers, "I've been watching you store away junk food."

Matthew looks down at the ground.

Mr. Martin continues. "Save some for me," and then he leaves to hand out balloons.

Glancing around to make sure that his mother is not looking, Matthew grabs another cupcake and rushes over to talk to Mrs. Nichols.

On the way he sees Amanda, who turns away from him and pretends he doesn't exist.

She and her friend laugh, meanly.

Matthew debates going over and doing something to embarrass her, like asking if she shops at Flat Chests R Us, but remembers that he promised his father not to fight with her. He thinks about how he's got to stop making promises and then he decides to keep going.

Rushing away, pretending that he never heard Amanda, he runs into Vanessa Singer, his worst enemy. Matthew literally runs into Vanessa, cupcake first.

Her brand-new T-shirt, which said "Born to Shop," now says "Born to hop" because marshmallow is covering part of it.

Chapter 3

Vanessa looks like she's going to hit the roof or, in this case, the sky . . . or Matthew.

Matthew is not sure what to do. He knows "I'm sorry" is not going to work. This is the Vanessa Singer who once started a group called G.E.T.H.I.M.—Girls Eager to Halt Immature Matthew. This is the Vanessa Singer who would like to see Matthew's name on the Ten Most Wanted List, to see him hunted down and put in solitary confinement so that she will never have to spend another day in school with him, not ever again.

The Vanessa Singer who wants him to graduate from high school and then college while he is in jail so that his diploma will read "P.U.—Prison University."

A crowd of sixth-graders starts to gather around them.

Matthew decides to try apologizing, even though he realizes that probably won't do any good.

After all it really was an accident.

"I'm sorry," he says.

Vanessa puts her hand on her hip. " 'I'm sorry' isn't good enough, bozo."

She thinks about all he has done to her and starts to list things. "Should I start with the gerbil in my Barbie lunchbox in second grade, or the note on my back in third grade that said "Cootie Motel," or the other eighty zillion things that you've done to me?"

She stamps her foot, which lands on Matthew's foot.

He hops up and down, yelling "Ow" and pretending she's broken it.

"Now look who's 'Born to hop' . . . and what are you going to do about the mess you've made of my new shirt?" She ignores his supposed pain.

"Why don't you offer to wipe it off her?" Mark Ellison jokes.

Matthew looks at where the icing has landed and can feel himself start to blush.

Vanessa yells at Matthew, "Try it and I'll knock your block off."

Matthew says, "I didn't say I was going to do that. I wouldn't want to touch you anyway, not with a ten-foot pole. Look, it was an accident. What do you want me to do? I'll buy you another stupid shirt. I've already said I'm sorry, that it was an accident."

One of their classmates, Ryma Browne, moves a little closer and softly says, "Come on, Vanessa. Why don't you turn the other cheek, let it go. It really was an accident."

Vanessa sneers, "Why should I turn the other cheek? This goofball would probably hit it with a pie."

Ryma backs off.

Vanessa, who cannot calm down once she gets angry at Matthew, yells, "You are such a pain."

Matthew stares at her.

He just doesn't know what to do.

He knows what he would like to do but he's not sure where he could find a rocket that would shoot Vanessa to Mars.

Mrs. Stanton, their teacher, walks up to them. "Vanessa, I saw what happened. Matthew didn't do it intentionally. . . . Although he really should have been watching more carefully. He's offered to buy you a new shirt . . . although I do believe it will all wash out. So what else do you want?"

What Vanessa really wants is for the whole thing to be over, for everyone not to be staring at them, for the icing not to be on her chest. But she doesn't know how to get out of this situation without seeming like she's backing down.

So she says, "I want Matthew to get detention for a month."

Mrs. Stanton sighs. "Vanessa. It's Saturday. Technically this is not school business. I just thought I could reason with you and try to work this out. I can't give anyone detention. And I really don't think this situation merits it."

Mrs. Stanton stares at her two students and wonders why she let herself get in the middle.

"I have an idea." Jil! Hudson, who changed the second *l* in her name to give herself more excitement and who loves getting people involved in doing things, comes forward. "I volunteered to help clean up at the end of the dedication. Maybe Matthew can help, to atone for his deed."

Matthew wonders what *atone* means, if it has something to do with music or body building, and then he remembers how Mrs. Stanton said that if you don't know a word, try to figure it out by the rest of the sentence or by the situation. He figures that he's really going to have to pay for this one . . . or die.

Vanessa frowns. She knows that Jil! and Matthew kind of like each other, so it's not going to be absolute torture. Still, the thought of Matthew having to deal with trash appeals to her since she thinks that "Matthew Martin" is another way of saying "garbage."

"Oh, okay." She gives in. "But if I can't get this clean, he's going to have to get me another one."

She walks away, feeling a little uncomfortable that she's turned everything into such a big deal but glad that Matthew is going to be stuck on the garbage detail.

"ATTENTION." A voice blares over the loudspeaker. "It's time for the ceremony to begin."

Everyone gathers around at the front of the playground area. There's a large crowd because building the playground was a real community effort. The design was done with the help of one of the parents who is an architect. The students helped to plan what was going into the playground.

Money was raised. Supplies were donated or bought at cost from community stores.

And then it was spring vacation. And everyone who could worked on the playground. Some built. Some watched the little kids of people who had other playground jobs. Some people served the food, which had been made by parents or donated by local restaurants and supermarkets. There were lots of jobs to do, and people worked day and night.

The mayor starts to speak, thanking all the people who helped, listing all the businesses, going on for a very long time.

Matthew puts his head on Jil!'s shoulder and pretends to snore.

It is the first time he has really done anything like that and he hopes that she doesn't think this means that they are engaged or something.

She giggles and then raps him lightly on his forehead with her knuckles. "Earth to Matthew. Wake up. Mrs. Nichols is going to speak."

Matthew looks up immediately.

Mrs. Nichols, the seventy-eight-year-old person the playground is being named after, is one of the people that Matthew likes best in the world. Not only is she a lot of fun, not only has she been a part of his family's life since he was born, not only does she make the best chocolate chip cookies in the world . . . but she is also an adult who really talks to kids and listens to them, not just asks dumb questions like "How old are you?" and "What grade are you in?"

Mrs. Nichols uses a cane to go to the microphone. She smiles and then speaks. "I have so much to be thankful for today. It's such an honor to have this wonderful playground named after me, and I can hardly wait until my hip is better and I can go down the slide and use the swings."

Many people laugh, thinking that she's joking.

Matthew, however, remembers how much she used to like going sledding with him and his friends and knows that she is serious.

She continues. "I am thankful that so many people have helped me."

Matthew remembers how, after she broke her hip, she almost had to sell her land to someone who wanted to turn it into a shopping center. He is thankful, too, that so many people helped her so that she didn't have to go away.

Mrs. Nichols concludes, "I am so proud to be part of a community that cares. Again, I thank you."

Matthew looks around.

Several people are crying, remembering how Mrs. Nichols has always helped, always volunteered at the school and church, always shared food from the farm with people who needed it, always offered good advice.

Everyone applauds when Mrs. Nichols finishes speaking.

After Mrs. Nichols is done, Mrs. Morgan, the principal, gets up to explain how the playground is for school use during the day and for community use after school and over the summer.

Then someone else explains how the next project will be to build a community recreation center on the property.

Matthew is beginning to think that the speeches are going to take longer than it took to get the playground built. He also remembers how much fun it was to plan and build the playground.

He thinks about how, by the time the speeches are done, the little kids are going to be adults.

Tuning out, Matthew looks around.

Ms. Klein, the media specialist, is rushing around filming everything.

As she points the camera in his direction, he crosses his eyes and puts his hands on both sides of his mouth and makes "fish lips."

Ms. Klein turns the camera away from him, so he looks to where his sister is standing with her boyfriend, Danny Cohen, and makes fish lips at her.

Amanda ignores him.

He notices that Vanessa is standing off by herself, pouting. The icing has come off and her T-shirt is wet. "Born to Shop" is back, although Matthew thought "Born to hop" was more appropriate and that "Born to Crab" would be even more appropriate.

He spots his parents, who are still in the guinea pig outfits. They have their arms around each other. In third grade there used to be guinea pigs in the classroom and they used to have babies practically every three minutes. Matthew hopes wearing those costumes does not give his parents ideas, since he thinks one sister is more than enough.

Putting his head back on Jil!'s shoulder, he starts to snore again. Getting bored with that sound, he starts to snort.

Jil! sighs and says, "How come it's never like this in the movies?" She then answers her own question. "That's probably because the movies are hardly ever about sixth-graders."

Matthew starts making chirping sounds and wonders if there are any cupcakes left at the refreshment table.

Finally the speeches are done and the little kids rush to use the playground, which looks like a magic wonderland.

Wood, ropes, and tires have been combined to form castles, pyramids, Viking ships, jungle mazes, and animal forms.

Matthew wonders what's going to happen next, now that the playground is completed.

"Clean up time," Jil! reminds him.

Matthew pretends that he doesn't hear Jil!, that he is intently watching some second-graders go through the tube slide.

Jil! raps him on the head with her knuckles, a method she has found that works with him and says, "Earth to Matthew. Pay attention."

He pretends to pick up a microphone on a spaceship communicator. "I'm up here in the clouds."

"I know. Your head is often up in the clouds." She

pretends to pick up the earth space-station communicator and says, "It is mission control's responsibility to make sure that even though you're up there, you can still come down to deal with the stuff on our planet. It's a tough job, but someone's got to do it. And anyway, if you don't, I have a feeling that this place is going to be littered with more than just this garbage . . . if Vanessa finds out that you got out of doing what you promised."

Matthew says, "I'm not afraid of Born-to-Hop Vanessa Singer, but I *did* promise, so I guess I'll land this vehicle." He continues pretending that he really is an astronaut. "Ground control. Get ready. I'm coming in for a landing. Ten . . . nine . . . eight . . . seven . . ."

He pretends to land.

Jil! hands him a biodegradable garbage bag. "Your assignment, sir, is to collect specimens of trash for further study and investigation."

Matthew looks at the bag and then at Jil!. "Couldn't my assignment be to check out the snack-eating habits of earthlings? Don't you need that information for your study?"

Jil! looks around the brand-new playground at all of the litter and shakes her head. "Your assignment as a humanoid is to help clean up the playground. Can't you hear it calling out to you? Earth to Matthew, Earth to Matthew."

Matthew puts his hand by his ear and bends down to the ground. "I think I can hear it. It's saying, 'Earth to Matthew, Earth to Matthew, how about some some

21

cupcakes . . . a frozen yogurt with M&M's on top, a banana split?' "

"Matthew." Jil! puts her hand on her hip.

"Jil!." Matthew puts his hand on his hip, imitating her. "If that's what the earth is calling out to me, to clean up garbage, my line is busy."

"Matthew, please." Jil! looks very unhappy.

Matthew feels a little confused. Back in the old days, at the beginning of sixth grade, he wouldn't have cared what Jil! thought, and he probably would have been one of the kids messing up the playground.

It's different now, somehow.

He wishes that earth had a computer so that he could send it a message: "Matthew to earth, Matthew to earth . . . What in the world is going on?"

Chapter 4

"Let's get this show on the road." Mrs. Stanton claps her hands, signaling that everyone in class should be seated. "We're getting ready to start a brand-new unit."

After everyone sits down, Matthew raises his hand. "Mrs. Stanton, I have a scientific question to ask you. It's about the animal kingdom."

"About your relatives, the apes?" Vanessa snickers.

"Vanessa." Mrs. Stanton uses the teacher voice that means, "Go one step further and you're in detention for two days."

Matthew makes monkey sounds at Vanessa—
"Chee-chee"—and then scratches himself and pretends
that he is picking fleas off his body and flicking them at
Vanessa.

"Matthew." Mrs. Stanton uses the teacher voice
that says, "And you're going to be joining her."

Matthew stops acting like a monkey and looks directly at Mrs. Stanton, giving her his best student look,
the one that says, "I'm not a bad kid. I'm just trying to
get through school in the only way I can, by joking
around a little. But don't forget that I still get good
grades, so don't get too angry at me."

Mrs. Stanton smiles. "Ask your question, Mr. Martin."

Matthew grins back. "You know how you're always saying that we should learn all we can about nature and how it works?"

Mrs. Stanton nods.

"Well," Matthew continues, "I have a question
about chickens."

Mrs. Stanton thinks, Perhaps he has read about the
recent outbreak of salmonella in eggs . . . or perhaps
it's one of those stupid chicken jokes he likes so much.
Either way, she thinks, I'll let him go for it.

Matthew grins again, showing his dimple. "Why
did the chicken cross the new playground?"

Shaking her head, Mrs. Stanton thinks about how
hard the class has been working and about how a few
minutes of joking is all right. "Mr. Martin, tell us. Why
did the chicken cross the new playground?"

"To get to the other slide" is the answer.

Some people groan.

Some laugh.

Vanessa Singer mumbles, "That's so funny, I forgot to laugh."

Jil! calls out, "That was a fowl joke."

Mrs. Stanton, who loves puns and encourages them in her classroom, says, "The delivery of that joke wasn't exactly poultry in motion."

Raising his hand, Joshua Jackson looks at her. "Eggsactly what did you mean by that? I thought that was an excellent yoke."

"An eggshellent joke. It broke me up." Lizzie Doran giggles.

"I don't want to be hard-boiled about this, but dozen everyone think it's time to get back to our regular class?" Mrs. Stanton calls the class to attention. "Now, let's get serious."

Matthew debates asking her who Serious is and why does she want to get him, but decides not to do it.

"Today we are going to begin a major study of the ecosystem," she informs them.

Matthew can't stop himself. Making it sound like he's calling out from a mountaintop, he says, "Today we are going to begin a major study of the echo-system . . . system . . . system . . . system."

"Enough." Mrs. Stanton grins, but uses the teacher voice that says, "Enough is enough is enough."

Everyone tries not to giggle.

She says nothing for a few minutes and then begins again. "The ecosystem, or the ecology system, is about how things in a specific area relate to each other and their environment. If something in nature changes or is disturbed, it affects every other part. If something harms the environment, such as a flood, that affects the people who live there, their health, their economy. It also concerns the people who may not live right there but who help them. It may cost them money, they may use their own resources. Another example is oil. If the oil supply in the Middle East is threatened because of politics, it affects every other part of the world. Prices go up. People may have to ration fuel. Businesses that use oil and gas will raise their prices, even though they don't directly sell those products. So you see, there is a lot that is interdependent. Life, economy, politics."

Matthew thinks about how science used to be so much easier to understand, how it was just one subject to study, and now it involves history, geography, math, and lots of other things.

Mrs. Stanton looks at everyone. "Who would like to give some other examples of how one thing environmentally affects something else?"

Vanessa is waving her hand wildly. "Me. Me. Me."

Like if Vanessa's parents got transferred to a different state, it would make me very happy, Matthew thinks.

"Like if someone, who will remain nameless, was absent from school, that would make me very happy, and then I would be in a good mood, and that would make Mrs. Stanton very happy, and then she might even decide to give the entire class A's for the day, except for that nameless absent person, and then everyone would be very happy. Isn't that what it would be like?" Vanessa smiles at her own explanation.

Matthew calls out, "Like if someone, who will remain nameless, was outside one day and a giant vulture swooped down, captured her, took her back to its nest, and the baby vultures ate her. Then the barfing baby birds fell out of the nest into the water and died, polluting the water with the disgustingness of the nameless person. Then the fish who got sick from the pollution got scooped up into a net and sold to the company that sells stuff to the school cafeteria. Then we all got sick from the polluted fish cakes. That's how it works, right?"

"I've warned everyone before, there is to be no making fun of anyone else in this class, no meanness toward each other, no name-calling." Mrs. Stanton says.

"I said 'the person who will remain nameless.'" Matthew and Vanessa say at the same time.

"You heard me." Mrs. Stanton takes out a piece of chalk. "Now, enough. To get back to the subject, you are both right: Ecosystems deal with how one thing affects another thing and then that affects something else. And it can continue."

"Ow, ow, ow" Jil! waves her hand. "I want to say something."

Matthew watches as Jil! practically jumps out of her seat.

He really likes the way she always gets so excited by things and wants to be involved.

Jil! says, "My mom is going to have a baby and she's decided to use a diaper service, not plastic diapers, unless absolutely necessary, because she did some research and found out that a baby can use eight to ten thousand diapers before it becomes fully toilet trained."

"Wow, that's a lot of you-know-what." Patrick Ryan holds his nose.

Jil! continues. "She found out that it takes the pulp from one tree to make five hundred diapers. So that comes to about twenty trees for each baby. Multiply that by the number of babies that use disposable diapers and we're wasting a lot of forests, and forests are important for a lot of reasons."

"My mom says that she loves disposable diapers, that in the old days it was a real mess." Ryma Browne makes a face.

"Do we have to talk about this gross stuff?" Zoe Alexander looks over at her boyfriend, Tyler White, whom she plans to marry and have two perfectly wonderful children with. She worries that if he listens to all of this, he may change his mind and take back the cubic zirconia ring he has given her. Since Zoe's mother has been married a lot and so has her father, she wants to get her own life settled as soon as possible.

Tyler is sitting at his desk pretending to look interested in the class conversation, but really thinking about how hungry he is and wondering what the cafeteria is serving today. He hopes it is not polluted fish cakes.

"I'm not done yet." Jil! jumps up and down. "And when my mother called the diaper company, she made sure that they don't use lots of chemicals to get the diapers really white. You know, stuff like chlorine bleach."

"That's expensive," Katie Delaney says. "Diaper services are expensive."

"So are disposable diapers. People can do the wash themselves."

"Yug." David Cohen looks at Mrs. Stanton. "Is this important? Do we have to talk about this? It has nothing to do with me. My mom says that there is no way that she's going to have any more babies, that there are enough children and stepchildren in our family."

"It does have something to do with you, with all of us," Lisa Levine tells David. "That's what the ecosystem is all about."

All about . . . about . . . about, thinks Matthew.

Mrs. Stanton explains. "I realize that we've used a lot of time to talk about diapers, but I think it's important. It's something that affects people worldwide."

"Yeah. It's something that everyone does." Brian Bruno laughs.

"Put a cork in it." Vanessa snarls at him. "You all act so immature sometimes."

"Maybe that's the answer." Brian laughs. "Someone should sell corks instead of diapers."

"Ugh."

Mrs. Stanton continues. "Part of every day, for the rest of the school year, will be spent working on this project. I'm going to break you up into groups and appoint a chairperson."

"Not Matthew," Brian calls out without thinking.

Everyone in class chuckles when they remember how Matthew as chairperson of the Mummy Committee got Brian encased in plaster and how Dr. Kellerman had to free him. Actually everyone but Brian is laughing. Everyone but Brian and Matthew.

They also remember the explosion when he was chairman of the Volcano Committee.

"I've chosen people who have not been chairperson yet, so that by the end of the year you will have all had the opportunity to exhibit your leadership qualities."

Katie Delaney squirms in her seat, knowing that she is going to be made chairman of a committee and not wanting to do it. She would rather just sit quietly and exercise her "followship qualities."

Mrs. Stanton passes out pieces of paper. "Here are the committee assignments. You will do group research on your topics and then work individually on your own project. Come up with some suggestions for changes that could be made worldwide and that we can do here in Califon, in your homes, at school. Suggestions that you can make to your parents and friends. You will also find out whether any of this is controversial, whether there are differences of opinion about anything."

Matthew looks down at the paper. Under "Recycling," he sees his name.

Katie Delaney is chairperson.

Tyler White is on the committee. So is Jil!.

Zoe frantically waves her hand. "Can we trade with someone? Please. Oh, please. You've put me on the Conserving Energy at Home Committee and what I'm really interested in is recycling."

What you're really interested in is Tyler, Matthew thinks.

Mrs. Stanton shakes her head. "The assignments are made. No changes will be made. Zoe, I'm sure that you will be a valuable asset to your committee and learn a lot."

Zoe pouts.

The only energy conservation at home that she cares about is not having her parents spend so much time marrying, divorcing, and dating.

Mrs. Stanton claps her hands. "To celebrate all the work that you will be doing on this unit, when we are finished, at the end of the year, at the end of the sixth grade, there will be a very special surprise trip for all of you who do your work. Remember, you must do your work or you won't be able to go."

Matthew and Joshua look at each other, remembering the adventure-book-report assignment.

Given permission to work together, they had played Nintendo instead of reading.

Panicking the night before the assignment was due, they decided to fake a book report. Matthew remembered a book that his mother talked about a lot because she thought Mr. Martin was like the main character.

From memory Matthew made up the story about this guy named Don, who acted a lot like a knight in shining armor. Matthew and Joshua turned in a report about a book called *Don Coyote,* written by Sir Vantays.

Mrs. Stanton informed them that the book was *Don Quixote* by Cervantes. She also informed them that they couldn't go on the class trip to McCarter Theatre.

They had to spend the entire day in the third-grade classroom while the rest of their class went to Princeton, New Jersey.

Mrs. Stanton also warned them that their next project had to be extra good if they wanted to go on the next trip.

And they want to go on the next trip.

* * *

"Where is the trip?" Pablo Martinez raises his hand.

"It wouldn't be a surprise if I told you. Trust me. You are all going to love it." Mrs. Stanton gathers up some papers on her desk. "Now, I want you all to separate into your groups and get started. Talk about your subject. Brainstorm. Then we'll go to the library and do some research."

There's a lot of noise as people start to move desks around.

Finally everyone is seated.

Matthew's group has gathered in the corner of the

room, next to the shelves of books that are available during free reading time.

Jil! passes a note to Matthew.

Hi!!! Lisa is having a party. Not this Saturday, but next Saturday night. Want to go together?
It doesn't have to be a real date, not if you don't want it to be.
But it could be if you want it to be. Or we could go separately. Or you could take Vanessa (just kidding). Or maybe you're busy.
Let me know during lunch. I'll be the one eating the peanut butter and banana sandwich.

Matthew looks at the note and then at Jil!, who seems to be a little embarrassed but also smiling.

He remembers how at the beginning of the school year he hated girls and wonders what has happened to change that. Except for Vanessa. And of course Amanda.

Katie says, "Well, I guess we should get started."

Matthew thinks she is referring to Jill's note and then realizes that she is talking about the recycling project.

Tyler starts talking about how he wants his project to be about how things should be recycled so that the space in landfills doesn't run out. He says, "My project will be called 'Down in the Dumps.'"

Matthew sits quietly for a change, wondering what he's going to tell Jill at lunch.

Chapter 5

"This will be just like old times." Mr. Martin pulls into a parking space at the circus fairgrounds.

"Boring." Amanda folds her arms and makes a face. "I can't believe that you made me come to this stupid thing when I could be at the mall with my friends."

Matthew sits in the backseat next to her and can't believe that they made her come either.

He also can't believe that he and his father didn't get to go to the carwash this morning because of this trip. He had really wanted to talk to his father about how he was going to Lisa's party with Jil!. There were a lot of questions he wanted to ask boy-to-man, and the next Boy-Bonding wouldn't be until the day of the party.

Tomorrow, Matthew thinks, I'll talk to him tomorrow or later tonight, if we get the chance to be alone.

"Boring." Amanda repeats.

"We're a family." Mr. Martin turns off the key in the ignition and turns around. "And we're going to act like a family. Now, let's get out of the car and have fun."

Amanda sighs and doesn't move.

Making his fish face at her, Matthew wonders why she has to ruin everything all the time, why she has to be an ecosystem disaster.

Turning around, Mrs. Martin says, "Come on. Give it a chance, Amanda. You know how much your father likes circuses, how much fun we used to have at them. This is what your father wanted for his birthday, so the least you can do is be gracious about it."

"I gave him a tie," Amanda sneers. "Isn't that enough? It's not fair that I can't get my allowance unless I do this."

Matthew steps on her foot as he gets out of the car. "Oops. Sorry about that."

"You did that intentionally," Amanda whines. "You didn't even have to be on my side of the car for any reason."

"Amanda. Out of the car . . . now." Mrs. Martin gets out of the car and opens Amanda's door. "And I mean now. Be reasonable. I hate it when you make me yell at you."

"So don't yell at me. Just let me lead my own life." Amanda gets out of the car and faces her mother.

Mr. Martin comes over. "Please. It's my birthday."

Amanda just stands there.

Matthew looks over at his parents, who look very upset.

He looks at Amanda, who also looks upset.

He can't figure out what's happening to his family. Sure, Amanda always acts like a pain, but not as bad as she's been acting lately. Before, everyone kind of got along. Sure, there were problems: His mother's fixation on health food, Amanda's being the oldest and getting to boss him around. But it was never Amanda who did stuff, it was usually Matthew "Trouble Is My Middle Name" Martin who did things. Like the time in first grade when he started a snot scrapbook, collected some from his friends, put it in the book, and labeled it, giving special sticker prizes to things like the longest one, the greenest, and the gooshiest. Or the time when Mrs. Stanton called home because he was spending all of his free time playing Super Mario and not doing his homework.

"Let's just have a good time." Mr. Martin reaches forward to rumple his daughter's hair, the way he always did when she was little.

"Don't touch my hair." Amanda backs away. "I really don't want to be here."

"You can either come with us or sit in the hot car," Mrs. Martin says.

"I'll sit in the car." Amanda gets into the car and closes the door.

"She could roast to death in there." Mr. Martin sounds worried.

"Only if we're lucky," Matthew says. "Come on. Let's go."

The three of them start to walk away.

The sun is very hot.

"I'm not sure that this is a good idea," Mrs. Martin says softly to her husband. "I'm not sure what we should do."

He puts his arm around her waist as they walk along. "I don't know either. Kids should be born with instruction manuals attached."

Walking alongside of them, Matthew says, "Did we come with warranties? Remember when my bike broke and the company had to fix it because the warranty wasn't up? Is there a warranty on Amanda? You could trade her in for another model."

"Stop talking about me." Amanda is walking right behind them. "It was too hot in the car. So I'm going to this stupid circus. Just don't expect me to have fun."

Matthew looks at her. He doesn't expect her to have fun. He does expect people to mistake her for one of the clowns the way she is dressed—wearing all black. Her pants are ripped and held together with safety pins. On her long black shirt she is wearing chains of skulls and bones, and her earrings are fluorescent green skulls. She is wearing makeup, a lot of makeup.

"Cotton candy." Mr. Martin pays for the tickets, spots the wagon selling junk food, and turns to his wife. "Remember, it's my birthday. The deal is no complaints about what we eat. Cotton candy . . . corn dogs . . . a cherry snow cone."

Matthew continues. "Popcorn . . . french fries . . . candy apples."

"I'm not holding anybody's head," Mrs. Martin informs them. "If you guys eat all that and throw up, you're on your own."

Matthew knows that isn't true. He knows he can always count on her, remembering when he made a brownie mix and ate all the dough without even baking it. She stayed up with him all night that time.

"Here you go, kid. Cotton candy." Mr. Martin hands his son a paper cone covered by the spun sugar.

"If any of my friends see me here, I'm just going to die," Amanda whines.

"If any of your friends see you here, Doofus, it's because they are here too." Matthew makes a mustache out of the cotton candy and places it on his lip. "Now, look, I'm getting sick of this. From now on the only sister I'm going to deal with is the one right here."

He points to the empty space right next to them. "This is my imaginary sister, Samanda. She's happy to be at the circus and to be part of this family. And from now on, until you turn human again, she's the only sister I have."

As the Martins enter the tent, Matthew is talking to the space next to him. "So, Samanda . . . how about a piece of cotton candy? Who do you think's going to win the World Series this year? Nice clothes you're wearing. I've always thought you looked good in

pink. Did you hear the joke about the bed? . . . No?
. . . Well, it hasn't been made yet."

When the Martins take their seats, Matthew makes
sure that a place is left for Samanda.

"He's just doing this to embarrass me," Amanda
informs everyone.

The lights dim.

And the circus begins.

Chapter 6

Matthew is sitting between Amanda and Samanda.

Amanda is sitting on his left, Samanda on his right, and his parents "next to" Samanda.

Mr. Martin is trying very hard not to sit on Samanda.

Matthew is trying very hard to ignore Amanda, who is sighing nonstop.

"There's not even a band at this bogus circus," Amanda observes. "Look at that. There's just one guy playing a drum set and the rest is coming from a com-

41

puter. This is so bogus. And so dinky. A circle of five rows of bleachers and they're not even totally filled up."

"Samanda. Isn't it nice that we're here at this nice little circus where it's not so big that there are bad seats? And that it's not too crowded on such a warm day?" Matthew pretends to talk to his "new sister."

The ringmaster introduces the first act. There are four birds that go up and down a small set of slides.

"Boring." Amanda yawns.

Matthew agrees but will not let her know that.

Mr. Martin informs them, "This is just a small family-run circus. Don't be too hard on it. It's fun, just not that big."

Someone comes on and foot-juggles things like kegs, logs, and flaming batons.

"I could be at the mall having a good time." Amanda makes a face and mumbles.

"You could be at the mall, giving grades to boys' butts. I see where you gave the new kid, Ned, a ninety-nine." Matthew grins at her.

"You've been reading my diary again. You little creep. You birdbrain." Amanda punches his arm.

Matthew turns to Samanda. "It's so nice that *you* are not a mall mole, that you spend your time reading, doing volunteer work, starting a group called SPCYB. Society for the Prevention of Cruelty to Younger Brothers. No *if*s, *and*s, or *butt*s about you."

"Twerp."

"And now, ladies and gentlemen and children of all ages," the ringmaster announces, "we must ask you to be absolutely quiet for our next act, brought to you from Paris, France . . . the Amazing Antoine, who will perform daring feats on the tightwire."

"That wire is no higher than a balance beam," Amanda observes.

Matthew disagrees. "It's about twice as high as that."

"Real daring." Amanda giggles. "If he falls off, he might break a toenail."

They watch as the guy jumps back and forth on the wire.

"Did the ringmaster say that the tightrope walker was going to do a daring feat or that he had daring feet, feet that dared him to do something?" Matthew puts his hand in Amanda's popcorn box.

She smiles and says, "Take some more if you want to."

Matthew looks at her and wonders if this is really his sister or if Amanda and Samanda have changed seats. He thinks of the old days when it really was fun to be with her and wonders how long her good mood will last.

There's a little applause when the act ends.

The clowns arrive, pretending to trip over things, squirting each other with make-believe flowers, and riding around in small cars.

Some of them run into the audience and start doing things to the people who are in the bleachers.

One of them with a big red nose, a squirting flower, polka-dotted pants, a striped shirt, and huge red shoes comes running up to where the Martin family is and discovers Amanda. He pantomimes putting his hand on his heart, as if he is falling in love with her. He bends his knee and acts as if he is proposing to her.

"Bug off," Amanda whispers.

He pulls paper flowers out of his sleeve and offers them to her.

Amanda is getting redder and redder as everyone looks at them and laughs.

"You quit that clowning around," she yells.

People around them start to laugh louder.

The clown puts his hands on his heart again.

Matthew hears Amanda whisper, "The only good clown is a dead clown."

Finally the clown leaves, pantomiming a broken heart.

Amanda sits there with her arms folded in front of her body, looking as if she's going to explode.

Matthew turns to her. "You should have accepted. Then you could have little clownettes."

"Shut up."

Matthew can't stop. "And if it didn't work out, people could say things to you like 'I told you not to marry that clown.'"

Mr. and Mrs. Martin start to laugh.

Amanda does explode. "It's no fair. You always think he's so funny. You don't even care about how embarrassing that was to me."

"Honey, calm down," Mr. Martin says. "Someday you'll look back on this and think it's very funny."

"Never." She stares straight ahead.

"Well, Samanda." Matthew looks to his right. "You liked the clowns, didn't you?"

He pretends to listen intently. "Oh, you love everything about the circus but you're getting a little hungry? What would you like? A hotdog, you say? And a soda? I'm sure that Dad would be glad to get it from that guy who is selling food."

"Haven't you had enough, honey?" Mrs. Martin asks her son.

"It's for Samanda."

Mr. Martin signals to the guy, who comes over to the side of the row and hands them the food, accidentally stepping on Amanda's feet as he passes the food over.

"Ouch," she yells.

"If you'd passed it to us, instead of sitting there with your arms folded, you wouldn't have gotten hurt," Matthew informs her.

"Shut up," she says once more.

During intermission Mr. Martin tries to act as if everything is going wonderfully.

He turns to Amanda and says, "Honey, I love clowns, but I can see why you might have gotten a little upset by that mime."

Amanda says, "I'm going to find the ladies' room."

"I didn't know it was missing." Matthew looks at her.

"Does this family have to turn everything into a joke?" Amanda sneers.

"I'll go with you." Mrs. Martin stands up.

"Oh, okay." Amanda sighs. "If you must."

As they leave, Mr. Martin looks at them and says, "I have a theory about why the lines at the ladies' rooms are much longer than the ones at the men's rooms. I think that it's because women often decide to accompany the other one, probably to talk about us."

Matthew looks at the empty space next to him. "Even Samanda went with them."

The ringmaster introduces "Antonio, the daring young man on the flying trapeze, from Rome, Italy."

Looking carefully, Matthew sees that Antonio from Italy is the same guy who was Antoine from France. The only difference is that he is wearing a new costume and a phony mustache.

Even his assistant is the same one, only now she's wearing a blond wig.

She looks like the person who was selling balloons at intermission.

Matthew wonders if later they are going to bring back another act, Anthony from Albany, who will be the same guy, but a juggler, with a beard.

No wonder Mr. Martin says that it's a family circus.

Family circuses are something that Matthew is beginning to understand.

With the way things are going, he's beginning to think that he lives in one.

Chapter 7

"My mother's going to have a cow when I tell her that balloons can be bad for the environment." Matthew shakes his head. "A cow? She's going to have a herd when she hears it. Part of her business is sending people out in costumes to deliver balloons to people."

"You've got to tell her." Jil! is adamant. "I read that the balloons that fly away sometimes break and end up in the water. Then fish, whales, and dolphins see it floating, think it's food, and swallow it. Then it can make them choke and die."

Matthew says, "The balloon industry says that's not true."

Jil! shrugs. "What else are they going to say, 'Buy a balloon, kill a creature'? Look, Matthew, we did a lot of research. There are two sides to just about every story, or at least manufacturers want you to think there are. I just think that you've got to tell your mother and have her make a decision."

Matthew thinks about how hard his mother has worked to build up her business, how she has finally started to make a profit. He also thinks about dead beached whales who have been found with plastic inside them. That also makes him think about how water creatures sometimes get caught in the rings that hold together six-packs, how they die. He's glad that his mother's business doesn't have to worry about that and thinks about how he's going to go home and remind his parents to cut the rings up before throwing them out.

"Life was much easier before we started studying all of this stuff." Matthew looks up from the book he is using for research on his subject: *Precycle Before You Have to Recycle.*

Katie Delaney holds up her notebook. "Look at all of the uses I've found for old panty hose: Tie it with a rubber band to an indoor vent pipe at the rear of the dryer and use it as a lint catcher. You can use the old panty hose to store the new panty hose, being sure to color-code it so that your pink holds pink and . . ."

Tyler and Matthew look at each other and start to laugh.

"I'll have to remember to do that to all of my panty

hose." Tyler is laughing so hard that he has to hold his stomach.

"That's probably what bank robbers do with the panty hose that they use as masks when they rob banks. They color-code them so that they can say, 'Today I'll wear my gray mask to go with my sweat suit.' " Matthew is also holding his stomach.

Jil! says, "Katie, just ignore these bozos."

Katie continues. "You can cover a broom with panty hose and dust walls and ceilings with it."

"Right. With the feet on it, the broom will walk around the room by itself." Matthew shakes his head.

"There's more." Katie shakes her finger at the boys. "Now, keep quiet. In the garden you can tie up bushes to fences. It'll blend in if you use the brown panty hose."

"It gives a whole new meaning to garden hose." Matthew is laughing so hard that his eyes are tearing.

"Cloth animals for kids to play with can be stuffed with old panty hose. You can cut up the legs into rings and use them as loops for weaving pot holders . . . after you dye them." Katie holds up her wrist. "And I made this bracelet out of those loops, to show how it can be done."

"That's really nice." Jil! looks at it.

"I made one for you too." Katie holds it up shyly.

Jil! grins, takes it, and puts it on.

Matthew picks up a pair of panty hose that Katie has brought in for her presentation.

Looking at it for a few minutes, he says, "Once I used a pair of these to find my sister, Amanda the

Hun's, contact lens. Attach one of these suckers to a vacuum hose and it'll help find the lens without doing anything to ruin it."

"That's very helpful." Jil! smiles at him. "We really are a good group."

Matthew puts the panty hose on his head so that the legs hang down over the sides of his face. "And you can do a rabbit imitation with them."

"Have those been used?" Tyler makes a face.

"By my mother. But they've been washed," Katie says.

Matthew pulls the panty hose off his head.

"And remember the Egypt unit," Jil! says, "how the girls cornrowed our hair and put the panty hose over our heads to keep our hair neat while we slept."

"Enough about panty hose for now," Matthew says. "Let's talk about the important stuff. What kind of food is Lisa going to have at her party?"

"Matthew." Katie, as chairperson of the committee, is trying to keep control. "We have to concentrate on our project."

"Am I going to have to gag your mouth with panty hose?" Jil! puts her hand over his mouth.

He lightly bites her hand.

Jil! checks for teeth marks.

"Are we going to play Pin the Panty Hose on the Donkey?" Matthew starts to laugh.

Katie starts to put away the two pairs of panty hose that she is planning to braid and turn into a dog leash.

"Wait. Give it to me for a minute." Matthew puts a

pair in each hand. "The pair in my right hand is Hose A. The one in my left hand is Hose B."

"Look." He holds up the pair in his left hand. "Hose B is much better than the other one—no way, Hose A."

Everyone groans and Katie wonders how she's going to get the group's report to be good enough so that everyone can go on the surprise trip that Mrs. Stanton is planning.

Chapter 8

"Matthew, you look very spiffy." Mrs. Martin looks proudly at her son.

"Oh, Mom." Matthew stares down at his high tops, which he's tied in honor of his first date.

"Very spiffy," Mrs. Martin repeats.

Wearing new jeans and a blue-and-white-striped polo shirt, Matthew stands in the living room, not feeling totally comfortable.

"I'll be glad to drive you to Jill's to pick her up and then drive you to the party. I'll even borrow the chauffeur costume from Mom's company." Mr. Martin grins.

"No. Please. Oh, no. Not the chauffeur's costume. Not a gorilla costume. Not a chicken costume. Nothing. I just want to walk over to Jil!'s, pick her up, and go to Lisa's," Matthew pleads. "It's too baby to have your parents drive you. And it's too weird to have parents in costumes when it's not even Halloween."

Mr. Martin looks at Mrs. Martin. "Drats. I was really looking forward to putting on that costume."

"Why don't you put it on anyway? I'll get dressed up in the princess costume and you can chauffeur me for pizza." Mrs. Martin grins. "I'll even put on my rhinestone tiara."

"You're going to do take-out, aren't you? Oh, please." Matthew is terrified that someone he knows will see them.

Mrs. Martin nods.

Amanda walks into the living room and says, in a challenging voice, "Like the way I've done my hair?"

Everyone stares at her.

Her hair has been colored black, with plum-colored highlights. One side is cut short. The other side is long. The back of her hair has been pulled into a ponytail.

"Well, I guess I better get going." Matthew doesn't want to hear his parents explode.

His mother is making little clicking noises in the back of her throat.

Matthew's not sure but he thinks he can hear his father start counting . . . one, two, three, four, five, six, seven, eight, nine . . .

Amanda smiles.

There's silence from both parents.

Matthew repeats, "Well, I better get going."

Mrs. Martin looks at her daughter and then at her husband.

Mr. Martin makes a motion that seems to say, "Stay calm. Don't give her the reaction she's looking for."

Mrs. Martin turns to Matthew. "Honey, have a wonderful time. Please call us when you're ready to leave. We really don't want you and Jil! to be walking home in the dark, late at night."

"Okay." Matthew nods, careful not to look at Amanda or to say anything to her.

Mrs. Martin looks like she's trying not to explode. She takes a deep breath and says, "Matthew, by the way, I want to let you know that I thought about what you said about the balloons being bad for the environment. I've decided to give them up and create gift baskets to present instead. They'll contain things like books and little items that have to do with the occasions being celebrated. Thanks for being so considerate and letting me know about that."

Matthew is going to remind her that she's already told him all about that and then he realizes that she's talking about it to stay calm and to mention how good he is being, in contrast to Amanda.

As Matthew leaves, he thinks about what a creep Amanda is and wonders if she's going to try out for a part in a horror film or if she's just trying to turn their house into a horror film.

He wishes he could hear what's going on in his

house right now and is also very glad that he's not there to hear it.

Walking away quickly, he starts to think about Jil! and how this is going to be his first date. What is it going to be like? How should he act when he picks her up? Should he kiss her good night at the end of the evening? What should he do in between those two events, the beginning and the end?

He only hopes that things go all right at Jil!'s house and that nothing embarrassing happens at the party.

Matthew thinks about it.

The bad news is that this is his very first date and he has no idea what to do.

The good news is that this is his very first date and he's never going to have another very first date again.

Chapter 9

"Okay, Matthew. Look this way and smile." Mr. Hudson points the video camera at Matthew and Jil!

"This is humiliating, absolutely humiliating. Totally and completely and absolutely humiliating." Jil! blushes and covers her face with her hands. "Matthew, I am sooooooooo sorry. He always does this. I can't stop him."

"Someday you're going to appreciate this." Mr. Hudson jumps up on a chair. "Now, look up here and smile. Jil!, take your hands away from your face."

Mrs. Hudson hands them a piece of cardboard, on which is printed:

FIRST DATE: JIL! AND MATTHEW MARTIN
SIXTH GRADE

"Okay, kids. Each of you hold on to the sign and look happy." Mr. Hudson films them.

"Dad. Please. That's enough." Jil! looks like she's going to cry. "Why didn't you make up a sign that says, "Last Date," because I'm never going out with anyone again, not ever, if this is the way you're going to be."

"Don't be so sensitive." Mr. Hudson starts filming from the top of Matthew's red hair to the bottom of his shoes.

Matthew's glad that he tied his shoes for a change.

"Matt doesn't mind, do you, Matt?" Mr. Hudson puts the camera down and looks at him.

"He does mind. He minds being filmed like this. And he minds being called Matt. His name is Matthew. Look, Dad. We have to go now."

"Wouldn't you like some milk and cookies first?" Mrs. Hudson offers.

Cookies, Matthew thinks. What a great idea.

"No." Jil! is emphatic. "If we have milk and cookies, then you'll take pictures of us eating, and that will be so yucky. You always wait until there's milk drool down my chin or crumbs and icing on my nose."

Matthew wonders what kind of cookies they are.

"Matt, I want to show you something." Mr. Hudson motions for him to follow.

"Dad, no." Jil! follows, too, since it is obvious that her father will not take no for an answer, even if Matthew had said no.

They go into a room with a wide-screen TV, six feet by six feet.

"Wow," Matthew says. "That would make for a really intense Nintendo game."

Lying on the couch is a boy of about six, who says, "Are you Matthew? Are you the guy who I'm not supposed to bother, who I'm not supposed to tell things to about Jil!? Jil! bribed me to stay in here."

"That's my brother, Jonathan. Ignore him." Jil! makes a face.

Mr. Hudson points to the wall opposite the television. "Now, Matt. Wait until you see this."

He opens some doors and shows that from floor to ceiling are shelves filled with videos. "Many of these are family videos. We have almost everything on camera, all of life's most important moments."

"Dad," Jil! pleads. "We have to go. I promised to help Lisa set up for the party."

Jonathan grins at Matthew, showing that his two front teeth are missing. "You should see the bathtub videos of Jil! from when she was little."

"Shut up." Jil! glares at him. "If you don't stop now, I won't give you the money I promised you."

"Then I'll tell him about all of the potty-training videos." Jonathan shrugs.

Matthew grins.

Listening to Jil! and Jonathan reminds him of the way he and Amanda fight.

Mr. Hudson puts his hand on Matthew's shoulder. "Matt, my boy, I've been taking videos since my in-laws gave us the camera when Mrs. Hudson and I got married."

Jil! is mumbling about how she wishes the camera had never been invented. Mrs. Hudson walks in, holding out a plate of sugar cookies. "Are you sure that I can't interest you in any of these?"

Matthew's hand is halfway to the plate when he hears Jil! say, "No. We really have to go."

Matthew withdraws his hand, cookieless.

As much as he wants a cookie, he realizes that he's got to be loyal to Jil! right now.

That's when he realizes that he must really like Jil!

Mr. Hudson pats his wife lightly on the stomach and continues. "For the new baby on the way, I've taken the hospital sonogram and spliced it to our tape. So our records will be even more complete."

"I'm just mortified." Jil! grabs Matthew's hand. "Come on. We've got to get out of here."

Matthew wants to ask Mr. Hudson if they've ever considered filming from the *very* beginning, but knows that there is no way he's going to say that out loud.

It does, however, make him smile, which Jil! sees.

She punches Matthew on the arm, pulls him out of the room, and yells to her parents, "We're going. Bye. See you later."

"Wait. I want to film you as you go out the door and down the sidewalk." Mr. Hudson rushes after them.

"Let's make a run for it," Jil! says.

"Do you think we could get away with mooning him?" Matthew whispers, thinking Jil! will say, "Oh, Matthew. You're so silly . . . and gross."

She shakes her head. "I used to do that when I was little. Now when company comes over, he shows them those pictures. He calls it 'Moon Over Califon.'"

As they rush off, they can hear Jonathan calling out, "Don't forget. You owe me money. I didn't show him the one where you barfed on the roller coaster."

"Race you to the end of the block." Jil! runs faster than Matthew has ever seen her move in gym class.

Once they round the corner and are out of sight of her father and his video camera, Jil! stops, holds her stomach, and catches her breath. "I am *mortified*. My family is just so embarrassing."

Matthew grins. "*Your* family is so embarrassing? Let me tell you about mine. At this very moment my parents are probably on their way out for pizza. My mother will be dressed as a princess, my father a chauffeur. And you should see what my sister has done to her hair. And you think your family is embarrassing!"

Jil! looks at Matthew and grins. "Maybe we should send my father over to your house to film it."

"Let's not and say we did." Matthew grins back. "Maybe we should just go over to Lisa's house and get this party started."

Chapter 10

"Lisa's cousin is so cute. So cute." Lizzie Doran keeps staring across the room at Simon. "I hope that I'm on his team."

"What do you mean, team?" Matthew puts a potato chip into his mouth.

"For the mystery-solving game that Lisa's parents planned," Lizzie explains, and then looks at Jil! "Isn't he just the cutest? Lisa says he's in the eighth grade. Don't you think older men who live in New York City are just so sophisticated?"

Matthew is trying to balance a potato chip on his nose.

"So sophisticated." Lizzie sighs. "Why didn't Lisa ever tell us that she has such a cute cousin?"

Jil! looks across the room at Simon, who she thinks looks okay but not as cute as Matthew. "Lizzie, she did tell us that she had an older boy cousin. Remember when she couldn't go to Jessica's pajama party because she had to go to Simon's bar mitzvah?"

"Oh, yeah, but she didn't say how cute he is . . . how cute and sophisticated . . . not like the boys in our class." Lizzie looks over to a section of the room where some boys are trying to teach Lisa's parrot some new vocabulary words.

Looking over at the boys, Matthew thinks how it would be fun to be with them but he's not sure whether he should go, since he and Jil! are dates.

"Maybe I should go over there and see what they are doing." Matthew sees how much fun his friends are having and thinks about how boring it is listening to Lizzie talk about how immature the Califon boys are.

"Have another potato chip." Jil! shoves the bowl under his nose.

"Don't mind if I do." Matthew grabs six chips, stuffs them in his mouth, and tries to whistle.

"Want anything else?" Jil! grins. "Like onion dip on your nose?"

Matthew grins back. "How about a book about the rules and regulations of sixth-grade dating?"

"It was already checked out of the library when I looked for it," Jil! kids.

Lisa claps her hands. "Okay, everyone. First of all I want you to know that this mystery search for refreshments is not my idea. My parents have decided that we will all have a simply wonderful time solving "The Case of the Missing Soda." It is *not,* I repeat *not,* my idea —but they are my parents and they paid for this party and they are at this very moment sitting upstairs in the kitchen with my aunt and uncle, waiting for this thing to start."

From across the room the bird squawks out one of the new words that it has just learned: "Barfola."

Lisa closes her eyes and says, "I'm never going to have a party again. Not until I'm out on my own and can have my own apartment and plan my own party."

"Relax," Jill! says. "We all have parents. At least your parents aren't using a video camera to record it."

"My parents would probably be lying on the recreation-room floor pretending to be dead, spattered with fake blood, or they'd be dressed up as cat burglars." Matthew thinks about how his parents love to get dressed up for things.

"It was a case of soda that was stolen, not a cat." Zoe is confused.

Matthew decides not to explain.

"At least your parents both do stuff with you. My parents won't do anything together, unless their lawyers are with them." Patrick Ryan thinks about the custody battle that has been going on, how his house is like an ecosystem . . . the Ryan ecosystem: The father leaves and it affects everything—the mother, the kids, the family budget, everyday routines. Sometimes Patrick feels like he's living in a rain forest, with all the crying that's been going on.

Patrick makes a face, feeling a little weird that he's said anything. He thinks about how he always pretends that it doesn't bother him and how his parents have told him that it's no one else's business what happens in their family.

Sarah looks at him, wishing that she could say something to help him since she's been through a bad divorce, too, and knows that everyone survived.

But she feels shy.

Lisa calls out, "First of all, we have to break into teams."

"I'm on Tyler's team," Zoe calls out.

"The lists are already made up," Lisa explains. "And yes, you and Tyler are on the same team."

"I promise to eat green vegetables for a year if Lisa's cousin is on my team," Lizzie whispers to Jil!

"You mean Allie?" Jil! teases, pointing to the third-grader who has been lurking near the boys who have been teaching the parrot new words.

"No! I don't mean Allie." Lizzie shakes her head.

Lisa says, "I'm going to call out the names right now and then each team will get a beginning clue. The clues for each team are different except for the last one. The team that finds the missing soda will receive free movie passes. And then we all get to drink the soda and eat the rest of the food. I am going to be on one of the teams because I don't want to hang around this house talking to my relatives while you're out looking for clues. Just know that I don't know where they hid the stupid soda. This is all my parents' idea and they set it up."

Lizzie keeps crossing her fingers and toes, hoping that Simon is on her team.

Lisa continues. "Team One will congregate by the television. Team Two by the tape deck. Now, here are the groups. It took me an hour to figure out these teams:"

Group One
Vanessa Singer
Zoe Alexander
Tyler White
Simon Bernstein
Billy Kellerman
Brian Bruno
Patrick Ryan
Katie Delaney
Ryma Browne
Sarah Montgomery
Lizzie Doran

Group Two
Matthew Martin
Jil! Hudson
Joshua Jackson
David Cohen
Pablo Martinez
Cathy Atwood
Jessica Weeks
Chloe Fulton

Mark Ellison
Lisa Levine
Allie Bernstein

Nobody complains about their group. Certainly
not Matthew, who is with Jil! and not with Vanessa,
who is glad she and Matthew are on different teams.
And very definitely there are no complaints from Lizzie
Doran.

People go to their assigned areas.

The groups are handed Polaroid pictures of the
missing case of soda as well as their first clues.

The groups sit around looking at the clues and fig-
uring out where they should go.

Matthew is sitting quietly, writing something
down.

"Any ideas?" Joshua asks him.

Matthew nods. "I have an idea for the name of the
group."

"We're supposed to be solving a mystery, not giving ourselves a name," Jil! reminds him.

He waves his hand. "Pay no attention to that
woman behind the curtain."

"This is not *The Wizard of Oz,* you know." Jil! shakes
her head.

Matthew, who loves to quote or misquote from his
favorite film, says, "Well, DoDo. I guess we're not in
Califon anymore. We're in Mystery Land, and it's time
to give the group a name, because all of my groups are
G.E.T.T.H.E.M. Here it is: Group Eager to Triumph
Handling Emerging Mysteries."

"Not bad." Pablo grins, thinking of Matthew's original group: Girls Easy to Torment Hopes Eager Matthew.

Once Group One hears that the other group has given themselves a name, they decide to use G.E.T.H.I.M. Originally Girls Eager to Halt Immature Matthew, it now becomes Geniuses Every Time Handle Important Mysteries.

And the mystery solving begins.

Chapter 11

Clue 1

You don't have to look far
It's where we sometimes
put the car
Look for where to "pick" up
the next clue

"The last line doesn't rhyme," Matthew says.

"No kidding, Sherlock." Mark makes a face.

"So where do we look? In the driveway? The garage? On the street? Those are the places your parents put the car," Pablo, who lives across the street, says.

"I vote for the garage," Lisa says.

"In New York City we park our car in a garage that is three blocks from where our apartment is," Allie tells them.

No one says anything for a minute.

Allie continues. "I know that no one wants me on their team because I'm only in third grade. But I couldn't be on the other team because that's where my brother is and he said that it was bad enough to have to be with 'little sixth-graders' and he didn't want to have to be on a team with his 'stupid kid sister.' So here I am. I just want you to know that in my third-grade class at P.S. 87, I am very popular and people actually like to have me on their team."

"Lighten up." Lisa looks at her cousin.

"We don't mind having you on our team." Cathy Atwood pats her on the head.

"I am not a dog." Allie looks up at her and grins.

"Let's get started." Joshua looks at his watch. "We don't want G.E.T.H.I.M. to beat us. Let's solve this clue and find . . . the case of the missing soda."

"The garage." David starts running toward it.

Everyone follows.

The garage is filled with lots of stored things—deflated basketballs, boxes of old clothes that Mrs. Levine is planning to donate to charity, unused bikes, garden tools, a guitar without strings, old tires, and Mr. Levine's railroad set.

"Okay." Lisa looks at everyone. "Now you know what secret slobs we all are."

"This looks neater than my room," Chloe says.

"Don't you want this anymore?" Allie holds up a Barbie cosmetic case.

"No." Lisa blushes. "You can have it."

Matthew continues to look at the clue. "The last line doesn't rhyme."

"Tell me something new." David starts searching in the railroad cars.

Matthew does not give up. *"Far . . . car . . . pick."*

Jil! stands behind him, puts her chin on his shoulder, and looks at the clue. "I don't get it."

Looking around the room, Matthew finally says, "Pick . . . you use a pick with a guitar. And *guitar* rhymes with *far* and *car*. . . . GUITAR."

Jil! and Matthew rush over to the guitar.

On the back is pinned a note.

"BINGO." Jil! yells.

"Elementary, my dear Hudson." Matthew thinks about all of the Sherlock Holmes films he and his father watch.

Clue 2
Go visit Mrs. Nichols.
She won't feed you
pickles.
This will be a clue
that tickles.

Lisa shakes her head. "And my parents are such sickles."

As G.E.T.T.H.E.M. rush out of the garage, they see G.E.T.H.I.M. heading in the opposite direction with their own clues.

"Let's make a run for it." Matthew doesn't care as much about winning the movie tickets as just winning.

The thought of Vanessa Singer having the chance to gloat is more than he can handle.

Arriving at Mrs. Nichols's farmhouse, they ring the bell.

She is ready for them, holding out a feather. "I understand you want something that tickles. Now, read the attached clue and I'll give you some chocolate chip cookies for the road."

Lisa says, "Thanks. Do you want to come over to our house later for cake? My mom said to let you know how much we'd all like that."

Mrs. Nichols looks at the group and smiles. "No. Thank you. This is a party for 'young folks' tonight. I'm just pleased to be part of the mystery hunt."

"You can sit upstairs with the old folks," Allie offers. "With my parents and my aunt and uncle."

"No. Thank you." Mrs. Nichols holds out the plate. "Please. Everyone have another cookie."

Matthew has trouble staying patient. "The clue. Let's read the clue."

Clue 3

Now that you have the quil!

Walk up the hil!

Check under the windowsil!

"Look at the explanation points," Jil! calls out.

"Exclamation points," Lisa reminds her.

"Whatever." Jil! shrugs. "The next clue must be at my house on the top of the hill."

"Bye," Mrs. Nichols calls out as everyone starts racing up the hill.

Matthew rushes down again and gives Mrs. Nichols a hug.

"Bye." He grins as Mrs. Nichols hands him two more cookies.

Quickly he catches up.

"I'm going to be mortified again." Jil! gasps from running and talking. "I just know that my father is going to be there with his stupid video camera."

G.E.T.T.H.E.M. arrives at the Hudson house.

Mr. Hudson is there, holding the camera. "Okay, kids. I want a group shot. Someone please stand in front holding this sign. How about you, the little one."

Allie, who he has pointed to, runs up to get the sign, which says,

THE CASE OF THE MISSING SODA
JIL!'S TEAM

"Mortified" is all that Jil! keeps repeating.

"Please, sir. We have to do this fast or the other team will beat us," Matthew tells him.

Once the pictures are taken, Mr. Hudson points to a window with an attached flower box. Under that windowsill is the clue.

Clue 4

Here's the final clue that
   your group seeks.
Let's hope that no soda
   leaks.
Go to the house that belongs
   to the family named

— — — — —

"My parents are such geeks." Lisa shakes her head.

Everyone looks at Jessica, whose last name is Weeks.

"So that's why my folks kept looking at each other and smiling." Jessica laughs. "I thought something was going on, I just couldn't figure out what."

"To the Weekses' house," Matthew yells. "And let's hurry. We don't want it to take months."

The race is on.

G.E.T.T.H.E.M. knows where the soda is and hopes that G.E.T.H.I.M. doesn't.

Everyone races to the Weekses' house.

They get to the door just as they see the group from G.E.T.T.H.E.M. rushing down the hill.

Matthew rings the bell and yells, "Ollie, ollie, in free. Everyone else has to pay."

"This isn't tag, bozo," Vanessa Singer yells as she races down the hill.

Mr. Weeks answers the doorbell and says, "It's around back."

The group of G.E.T.T.H.E.M. gets to the soda first.

The case is sitting in a little red wagon, ready to be taken back to the Levine home.

Matthew grabs the handle and yells, "We win."

"Drats." Tyler White sinks to the ground exhausted.

So does Zoe.

So does everyone else.

"That was fun," Billy Kellerman says. "I thought it was going to be doofy, but it was fun."

Lisa agrees. "It was. But don't tell my parents. They'll just say 'I told you so' to me."

Mr. and Mrs. Weeks come out to their backyard and look at the twenty-two people sprawled out on their lawn.

Mr. Weeks announces, "The Levines have one more rhyme for you and here it is:

"The first group will get movie passes
But because we don't want any sad lads and lasses
So will the group in second place
Because we don't want winners and losers in this race."

"Bad rhyme. Good idea," David Cohen says.

"You know what this means." Chloe jumps up. "We can all go to the movies next week. Then we'll go to my house for ice cream sundaes."

Everyone cheers and heads back to Lisa's to continue the party.

Chapter 12

"I'm so proud of you." Mrs. Stanton beams at her class.

"It's not always easy." Zoe raises her hand. "I tried to explain to my mother about how much water we could save if she didn't use the bathtub so much, if she took showers instead. But she didn't want to listen. She said that long baths are relaxation for her and she's not willing to give them up."

Ryma turns to Zoe. "Maybe you can get her to do some of the other things to save water. You could use less water in your toilet tank by putting in a plastic bottle filled with water and some stones. Doing this will also recycle small juice bottles or dishwashing soap bottles. You can save one to two gallons per flush."

"If kings and queens did that with their toilets, it would be a royal flush," David Cohen jokes.

Ryma ignores David. "Zoe, ask your mother if she'd give up even one bath a week and take a shower instead."

"I'll try." Zoe sighs.

"My parents bought a special low-flow shower-head that uses much less water," Vanessa informs everyone.

Matthew looks at Vanessa and wishes that she had taken a low-flow shower and gone down the drain to Siberia.

Matthew then looks at Jil! and smiles.

She is wearing a gray skirt, a pink shirt, a pair of pink socks over gray ones, and lots of rhinestone jewelry. Her shoes are tied with hot pink, sparkly laces. Her brown hair is held up with a rhinestone clip.

It's the first time Matthew has ever noticed a girl's clothes and cared.

Matthew thinks about Lisa's party and how his parents picked up him and Jil! afterward to drive them home. He remembers how he walked Jil! up to the door and how they stood in the doorway in such a way that his parents couldn't see them from the car. He remembers how, just as he was going to give Jil! a kiss, his first kiss, her first kiss, their first kiss, the front door slowly opened and Mr. Hudson walked out, pointing the camera at them.

Matthew looks at Jil! and wonders what it would be like if he had actually kissed her and whether his bubble gum would have ended up in her mouth.

Jil! is frantically waving her hand. "Ow. Ow. Ow."

"Jil!." Mrs. Stanton calls on her.

"Even though my father usually totally embarrasses me, the other day he showed me a good way to check for water leaks. He said to put twelve drops of either red or blue food coloring into the toilet tank. So I put in red because, with the water, it would dilute and become my favorite color, pink. Then we waited fifteen minutes to see if there was any color in the toilet. If there had been, then there would have been a leak." She giggles. "If anyone wants to see it, you can. He took a video of it. In some houses they watch the Rose Bowl and the Orange Bowl. In our house we watch the Toilet Bowl."

"Has anyone else noticed how much time we've spent talking about stuff like toilets and diapers and stuff?" Cathy scrunches her nose.

Mrs. Stanton says, "Do you think that all of this talk is a *waste?*"

Cathy shakes her head. "No. But I would like to mention something that our group is going to do that does not deal with waste. We did a lot of research about wild life, so we called a zoo, pooled our money, and joined their Adopt an Animal program."

"That's really terrific." Mrs. Stanton claps her hands.

Lisa said, "Our group has a couple of wonderful ideas. We want to do some work on Mrs. Nichols's property."

"It's not just hers anymore," Mrs. Stanton reminds them. "We need to get permission from the conservancy. What do you want to do?"

Lisa counts on her fingers. "One: We want to plant some trees. Two: We want to take some of the usable garbage from the school cafeteria and use it to make a compost heap. Three: We want to plant things on the property that we can use in the cafeteria. We can use the compost to help make the things grow. If the school can't use the food because of rules or something, then we can give what we grow to some poor people who need it."

"I'm very proud of you." Mrs. Stanton beams.

Mark Ellison raises his hand. "Our group wants to try a one-day experiment. We want everyone in this class to give up using electrical things. No blow dryer."

"No blow dryer!" Zoe yells. "No way. I look terrible if I can't dry my hair."

"You'll look fine," Tyler says.

"My mother told me that no woman should ever be seen without makeup on and her hair neatly in place," Zoe informs everyone.

"Aarg" is Jil!'s comment.

Mark continues. "No curling iron, no electric toothbrush, no can opener, no toaster, no electric juicer, no microwave, no TV."

"No TV," Joshua yells. "No fair."

"No Nintendo." Matthew pretends to be someone

they studied about in history class. "Give me Nintendo or give me death."

"No electric Water Pik." Mark looks at everyone. "Come on. It's not forever. It's only for one day. It's to show us how much electricity we use on unnecessary things."

"Nintendo is not unnecessary," Matthew mumbles.

"Actually my dentist thinks that the tooth appliances are important, so maybe we should take that off the list," Mrs. Stanton tells them.

"Oh, okay," Mark says. "But I really think you could floss. One day. It's not going to kill you. Let's all take a vote. All in favor, say 'Aye.' "

There are several sighs.

Zoe can be heard softly saying, "No blow dryer. Civilization will never be the same."

"One day. Think of what it will mean to the environment," Mark pleads. "And we can ask other classes to do this too."

There's silence for a minute and then Mark says, "All in favor, say 'Aye.' "

Everyone says, "Aye," although it sounds like Zoe is saying "Aye-yaye-yaye."

Mrs. Stanton claps her hands once more. "You are truly a terrific class. I'm very proud of you."

Matthew grins. He's already given his report on precycling, talking about buying things that can be recycled or are already made from recycled materials. He's talked about buying toys that are not overly packaged or badly made.

The class voted and chose his computer design for the tote bag that they are planning to have made and sell to people to use and reuse, instead of plastic and paper bags. Profits will be donated to help save the rain forest.

Matthew's happy because Mrs. Stanton has already said that he can go on the trip, that everyone can go.

There's only one problem that Matthew has had, and that was trying to convince everyone to use lunchboxes, Thermoses, and reusable storage containers instead of paper and plastic bags.

"Too doofy." "Only babies carry lunchboxes." "I'd die before anyone ever saw me carrying a lunchbox." "Get real, Matthew." "The seventh- and eighth-graders would make fun of us." These were some of the responses.

Actually no one in the class would bring a lunchbox, even if they were hypnotized, not even Matthew.

The only person that he's convinced to use a lunchbox is his father, who now carries an ancient Howdy Doody one to work.

The bell rings, signaling the beginning of lunch.

Before Mrs. Stanton dismisses them, she says, "After lunch I'm going to announce where we will be going for our trip so that we can start to make arrangements."

The trip.

Everyone's been guessing. Washington, D.C., Disney World, Paris, Action Park, the Califon Pond.

After lunch seems like such a long time.

It makes Matthew think of his favorite fourth-grade joke. Question: How do you keep a turkey in suspense? Answer: I'll tell you later.

"Can't you tell us now? Oh, please. Oh, please." Jil! waves her hand.

Mrs. Stanton shakes her head and grins. "After lunch. Class dismissed."

It's the first time all year that everyone in class can't wait for lunch to be over.

Chapter 13

I hope it's Disney World, Matthew thinks as the class sits down.

Everyone's excited.

Mrs. Stanton sits on her desk.

Everyone waits quietly for her to speak.

"We're going to a very special program run by The Franklin Institute in Philadelphia, Pennsylvania," she tells them.

"I've been there," several of her students say at the same time.

"I was hoping for Disney World." Matthew is disappointed, even though he really knew that there was no real chance for that hope.

"Action Park. I wanted to go on all of the rides." David makes a face. "Drats."

"This is special," Mrs. Stanton says. "The program is called Camp-In. We not only go to special programs, we also get to spend the entire night in the museum. It's a terrific program."

"Do they have a room with beds?"

"Is it just us?"

"Do our parents have to chaperon? And if so, can they be banned from bringing video cameras?"

"What kind of food will they have for us to eat?"

"When are we going?"

Mrs. Stanton holds up her hands. "Enough questions for now. We'll be going in three weeks. It will be our last major activity before summer vacation."

"Can I bring my hair dryer to Camp-In?" Zoe raises her hand. "And where are we all going to sleep?"

Mrs. Stanton informs her, "No hair dryers allowed. Also no hair spray."

"The aerosol ones are bad for the environment anyway." Cathy Atwood has been doing her research.

As Mrs. Stanton passes out permission slips, she says, "You don't have to memorize all of what I am telling you, because the information is on the sheet of paper with the permission slip. I'm just going over all of this so that you will know the procedure. The week before we go I will remind you of everything.

"Now, here are some of the facts. On the Friday

that we're going, the buses will pick us up after school right in front.

"Each of us is to bring a sleeping bag, a toothbrush, toothpaste, a washcloth, and a plastic bag or duffle bag large enough for all of these items. If you use a plastic bag, don't forget to recycle it. Also you will bring a packed dinner, unless you want to buy something from the cafeteria there."

"Do you think we could have pizzas delivered to the museum?" Matthew asks.

"Extra cheese and pepperoni on mine." Joshua is practically drooling.

"No pizza delivery for students." Mrs. Stanton decides not to let them know that adults have a delivery made to their leaders' lounge. "They will supply a snack to you at night and at breakfast.

"You must label the plastic bag with your name and the name of the school. You are not to bring pajamas!!! We will be sleeping in the clothes that we wore that day."

"And then we'll be wearing the same clothes the next day? Gross." The girls make faces.

"What's the big deal?" Matthew asks.

"Will it be just our group in the museum?" Sarah asks.

"No," Mrs. Stanton says. "There will be all sorts of groups there. School groups, Boy Scout and Girl Scout troops, church youth fellowships."

"Where are we going to sleep? Are we going to have our own room? Are we going to have to sleep in a room with strangers?" Sarah looks concerned.

"Several of the rooms in the museum are used for sleeping. Each group will be assigned to a room. There will be other groups in the room also, but we'll have our own section." Mrs. Stanton looks at everyone. "Don't worry. This will be fun, sort of like a giant pajama party, only no pajamas."

Someone starts to snicker.

"Enough." Mrs. Stanton frowns. "You know what I mean. . . . A pajama party with clothes *on.* . . . Look, this is going to be wonderful. Does anyone have any concerns?"

"What if someone snores all night and I can't sleep?" Vanessa is worried. "What if someone has nightmares?"

"You are a nightmare," Matthew wants to say, but doesn't.

"It's only one night," Mrs. Stanton explains. "It will be all right."

"Do parents have to chaperon?" Jil! can just imagine her father videotaping this one.

Mrs. Stanton nods. "There has to be a chaperon for every eight children."

"I'm not a child. I'm a young adult." Matthew tries to look mature.

"You're a child," Vanessa wants to say, but doesn't.

"There are twenty students in this class and I'm bringing my own little girl, Marie. It would be a good idea to have three parents as chaperons. Ask your parents who would like to come. It does cost something for everyone, so be sure to bring in your money with the permission slip. If anyone has a problem about the money, be sure to speak to me privately. Everyone will be able to go on this trip. Don't worry."

"This is going to be so fun." Jil! grins widely.

"A coed pajama party. I'm not sure that my parents are going to approve." Sarah looks worried.

"I'll talk to them," Mrs. Stanton says. "I'll explain that it's a sleep-over in a museum with lectures, classes, and films—and a show at the planetarium."

Ryma raises her hand. "Over that weekend I'm supposed to go to my father's house. It's his joint-custody time."

"Talk to him. See if he wants to be one of the chaperons." Mrs. Stanton stands up.

Ryma grins as she thinks of her father sleeping on the floor of a museum . . . her father, who once said that his idea of camping out was not staying at the Ritz Hotel.

"We were sort of hoping for Disney World or Paris," Matthew tells her.

Mrs. Stanton shakes her head and laughs. "Maybe for your seventh-grade trip. You can ask Mr. Arnold when you get to his class."

"If we can't go to Disney World or Paris," Matthew says, grinning, "The Franklin Institute sounds great to me."

Everyone agrees as Mrs. Stanton starts to talk about all the things there: the Futures Center, the exhibits about the things that they have been studying, the Omniverse film, the gift shop.

"I just can't wait." Jil! repeats.

Three weeks seems too far away.

Chapter 14

"Boy-Bonding Time." Mr. Martin stands at the bottom of the steps and calls upstairs. "Let's get a move on."

Matthew bounds downstairs, three steps at a time.

Mrs. Martin comes into the living room. "Are you two in training for the Olympic noise-making event?"

Both Martin males yell in unison, "Boy-Bonding Time."

Mrs. Martin laughs. "I get it. You're actually in training for the synchronized yelling competition, the one guaranteed to drive mothers and wives nuts."

Mr. Martin whispers something to Matthew.

Both of them pretend to do the backstroke, circling around Mrs. Martin.

"Enough already," she yells as they lie down on the floor, lifting their legs and pretending to be synchronized swimmers.

Matthew and his father look at each other and laugh.

Mrs. Martin looks down at them and shakes her head.

The front door opens and Amanda walks in.

She looks down at her father and brother and gasps. "Is everything all right?"

Her father jumps up. "Everything's fine, honey. Don't worry. We're just fooling around."

Matthew lies on the floor, continuing to kick his leg. "And now it's time for the individual synchronized swimming. Although how can it be individual when it's supposed to be something that's done together?"

Mrs. Martin looks at Amanda. "Why do you have that scarf on your head when it's springtime? What do you have on your nose? Oh, Amanda . . . What have you done to yourself this time?"

Matthew jumps up and looks closely at his sister, who is wearing a nose ring. "You got your nose pierced. Ow . . . how gross!"

Mrs. Martin walks up to her daughter. "Amanda, I want you to take off that scarf."

Amanda puts her hands to her head. "No. I don't have to."

Mr. and Mrs. Martin exchange looks.

"Do what your mother says." Mr. Martin sounds stern.

Matthew looks up his sister's nose. "What happens when you have to blow your nose? Does the snot get caught in the ring? Did it hurt to have your nose pierced? When you take out the ring, does the snot come out of the hole?"

"Matthew. Go upstairs. Right now." His mother points to the staircase.

"No fair," Matthew yells. "It's my house too. And I didn't do anything wrong."

"Upstairs," his father says softly.

"What happened to Boy-Bonding Time?" Matthew stamps his foot. "How come she gets to ruin everything? And what do you care what she's done to her hair this time? She's always dying it some stupid color. This time she's probably done it black with a white stripe . . . so that she looks like the skunk that she is."

"I did not." Amanda interrupts. "I didn't dye it this time."

Everyone looks at Amanda, as she takes off the scarf.

She has shaved off her hair and is totally bald.

Mrs. Martin gasps and starts to cry.

Mr. Martin shuts his eyes.

For once Matthew does not make a remark.

Amanda looks at her family.

They look at the Amanda who used to have beautiful blond hair . . . who used to have a nostril without a nose ring attached . . . who used to smile and laugh.

Now they see an Amanda who is totally bald, an Amanda who is wearing a nose ring, who is glaring at them.

"Honey, why?" Mrs. Martin says softly, trying not to cry.

"Because," Amanda says.

"You can't go out looking like that." Her mother shakes her head.

"Why not? It's my life. I can look any way I want to look." Amanda stamps her foot.

"But you look terrible," Mr. Martin says softly. "You used to be so pretty."

Amanda starts to yell. "It's my life. I can do what I want to do with it."

Mr. Martin yells back. "You are thirteen years old. As long as you live in this house, you have to listen to us. . . . I don't get it. We're good parents. We care about our children. We only want what is best for them. Why have you done this to us?"

Mrs. Martin reaches out to touch Amanda's head. "Honey."

"Leave me alone," Amanda yells.

"What's going on? What's wrong?" Mrs. Martin is trying to be calm and understand what is going on in her daughter's head.

"I got tired of looking like everyone else. I want my life to be more exciting. On MTV I saw someone who looked really terrific with her head shaved, so I decided to try it." Amanda takes a compact out of her backpack and looks in the mirror.

She starts to cry.

Her mother starts to hug her.

Amanda backs off. "Stop being so understanding. Why can't you just leave me alone?"

Mrs. Martin backs off. "Amanda, I don't know what to do. You get angry at me if you think I don't understand. You get angry at me if I am too understanding. I've tried so hard to be the kind of mother you can come to, to be a good mother. I've tried so hard not to make the same mistakes that my mother did with me. And nothing works. You're angry all the time. Nothing we do pleases you."

Amanda stands quietly.

Matthew thinks about how he really wants to slug her.

Mr. Martin softly says, "Is there something we need to know? Can we help you? I have to ask you this: Are you taking drugs? Is there a problem with someone at school? What is going on?"

Amanda gasps. "I don't take drugs. How can you think that about me? How stupid do you think I am?"

Stupid enough to shave all the hair off your head, Matthew thinks.

"I have to ask." Mr. Martin looks at his daughter. "You must admit that you've been acting very different lately."

Amanda stands there, looking in the mirror.

A tear trickles down her face.

This time Mrs. Martin does go up to her daughter and hugs her, and this time Amanda does not push her away.

Amanda starts to cry.

Mrs. Martin just holds her.

Mr. Martin walks up to them and puts his arms around both of them.

Matthew's not sure whether or not he wants to murder Amanda for causing all this trouble, for getting all this attention, for always messing up the time that he wants to spend with his father.

He's not sure if he wants to try to understand what Amanda is going through, if he can figure out some way to help his sister.

He's not sure if he should shave his own head to get some more attention.

Life in the Martin house is getting very confusing.

Amanda pulls away from her parents and looks at them. "I just want things to be different, to not be so boring. I want to be more grown up and make my own decisions."

Her parents stand quietly, letting her continue.

She touches the top of her head. "I'm never going back to school again—not until my hair grows back."

Mr. Martin shakes his head. "No way, kiddo. Hair or no hair, you have to go to school."

Mrs. Martin puts her hand on her husband's arm. "Honey, why don't you and Matthew go out now? Amanda and I will do some talking and then she and I will go out shopping for a wig."

Putting a paper bag over her head will be cheaper, Matthew thinks.

Amanda continues to cry.

She keeps sniffling.

Mr. Martin hands her a tissue.

Matthew checks to see if the nose ring catches what is coming out of her nose.

Amanda removes the nose ring.

Matthew sees that her nose isn't really pierced, that the nose ring just makes it look that way.

His parents notice that, too, and are very relieved.

They all look at her head, hoping that somehow it wasn't really shaved after all.

There are tiny hair bristles and nicks all over her head.

Mrs. Martin puts her hand on her husband's arm again. "Why don't you and Matthew go out now that things are under control?"

Mr. Martin looks at his daughter, wondering if things are really under control, if they ever will be again.

Then he looks at Matthew, who is standing there, looking like he's landed on another planet.

Mr. Martin goes up to Matthew and puts his arm around his shoulders. "It's Boy-Bonding Time, son. Let's go."

Chapter 15

"Fore," Matthew yells as his golf ball goes into the rabbit's mouth.

"Five," Mr. Martin yells as his golf ball hits the rabbit on its forehead and falls back onto the imitation turf.

"I thought you were supposed to yell 'Fore' when you hit the ball." Matthew putts into the hole and marks down his score, 3.

Mr. Martin picks up his golf ball, walks up to the rabbit's mouth, and throws the ball to the other side of miniature-golf-hole 6. "I called out 'five' because you called out 'four,' and five comes after four. And anyway my score for this hole is five."

Matthew shakes his head. "No way, José. You hit that ball at least eight times . . . and I said 'fore,' not 'four.' "

"Duck," Mr. Martin yells.

Matthew looks at his father. "Actually it's not duck, it's chicken. The next course has a chicken that you have to go through, so that it looks like the chicken is laying the golf ball like an egg."

"No, I mean duck. I'm getting ready to hit this ball and I'm afraid that it's going to hit you. So, duck." Mr. Martin grins.

Matthew ducks.

Mr. Martin's golf ball never leaves the ground, going straight into the hole.

"I ducked for nothing," Matthew calls out.

Putting his arm around his son's shoulders, Mr. Martin says, "Remember the good old days . . . like last week, when we used to go to the carwash and duck when the machines went over the car."

Matthew sighs. "Yes. I remember the good old days."

Both stand quietly for a minute remembering the fun at the carwash.

"Sometimes I wish that we'd never studied ecology." Matthew shakes his head. "Then I would never have learned how much water gets wasted in a carwash, how we're supposed to use a bucket and sponges instead."

"It's not always easy to do the right thing when the other way is much less work and much more fun," Mr. Martin says. "But look at the bright side . . . look at all the other things we can still do: miniature golf, batting practice, racing cars."

Matthew hits his golf ball into the middle of a windmill. It goes through and rolls right up next to the hole. He goes up to his father and says, "Slap me five."

His father slaps palms with him and yells, "Fore."

At the last hole they try to get the ball into the clown's mouth for a free game.

Missing, they look at each other and shrug.

"On to the batting cage?" Mr. Martin suggests.

Matthew nods. "Let's use the major-league speed."

Mr. Martin nods back.

Matthew continues. "And I'll pretend that the ball is my sister's bald head and I'll hit it as hard as I can."

"A little angry, huh?" Mr. Martin looks at his son. "I think that we're going to have to talk about this, even though I wish we didn't have to because I'm not sure of what to say."

"You're the grown-up." Matthew looks at him.

Taking the golf club from his son and giving both clubs to the attendant, Mr. Martin is silent for a minute. Then he turns to Matthew and says, "How about getting some soft ice cream and sitting down and talking for a bit?"

"Chocolate-vanilla swirl with rainbow sprinkles?" Matthew asks.

"It's a deal."

Once the ice cream is bought, Matthew and Mr. Martin sit at a table under a huge sun umbrella.

Matthew uses his tongue to make paths in the ice cream.

Mr. Martin stares at his cone for a minute. It's also a swirl but with chocolate sprinkles. "I just have to check to make sure that none of these move, that none of these are ants. When I was little, my mother always used to tell me about the time my aunt saw some sprinkles in a dish, licked her finger, and stuck it into the dish. As she put her finger into her mouth, she saw something move in the plate. It was some ants that had gotten into the food."

"Arg." Matthew makes a face. "An ant-eating aunt."

Mr. Martin continues checking. "The coast is clear."

He takes a bite of his cone.

Matthew starts to slurp his ice cream.

"About Amanda . . ." Mr. Martin starts. "I know that all of this fuss is not easy for you."

Matthew shrugs. "Who cares?"

"Obviously you do if you want to pretend the baseball is her head."

"Her bald head," Matthew reminds him.

"Don't remind me." Mr. Martin holds the ice cream away because it is starting to drip.

"Amanda is a pain," Matthew informs his father.

"Amanda is going through a difficult time," his father informs him.

"Amanda is a pain. And she is making my life a

pain." Matthew makes a face. "It used to be so different in the house."

"Amanda is going through a difficult time and as a result we are all going through a rough time. Your mother and I have discussed it and we've decided to get some family counseling to try to help us. We would like you to get some counseling, too, since this also affects you." Mr. Martin looks at his son. "How do you feel about that?"

"I don't need counseling." Matthew glares at his father.

"I guess I wasn't very clear. We don't want you to get individual counseling, but we do want you to be there for family counseling." Mr. Martin shakes his head. "Amanda's clearly not happy. Your mother and I are not sure how best to handle the situation. This is something we have to do as a family to help each other."

"Oh, okay." Matthew shrugs. "I just want things to go back to the way they were."

"Me too. But I don't think that's possible." His father looks unhappy. "We all have to work at making things better with the way that things really are, not the way we wish they were."

"But it's not my fault." Matthew looks angry. "It's Amanda's problem and she's making it mine . . . ours."

Mr. Martin continues. "It is our family's problem. . . . Maybe there are some things that have caused Amanda to act this way. I don't know. What I do know is that we have a problem and we all have to work on it.

And who knows, maybe soon Amanda will be able to work this all out of her system."

"System . . . system . . . system. . . ." Matthew thinks again about what he has been learning in school.

"So we all work together at this. It's a deal?" Mr. Martin stares at his son.

"Deal." Matthew starts to shake hands until he realizes that his hand is covered with ice cream.

Mr. Martin grabs the hand and shakes it anyway.

Chapter 16

The bus pulls up and stops in front of the Twentieth Street entrance of The Franklin Institute at 6:00 P.M.

"Right on time." Mrs. Stanton stands up in the front of the bus, right next to the driver's seat. "I have a few announcements to make before we get off the bus."

Mr. Hudson starts filming her.

"Why couldn't he have stayed home?" Jil! whispers to Matthew, who is sitting next to her on the bus. "Why couldn't my mother have stayed home? She's three months pregnant. Doesn't the baby need to sleep in a bed? Why did they have to bring Jonathan? Why do they see the word *chaperon* on the permission slip and think it means the family of Jil! Hudson? Why doesn't that camera break?"

Matthew is impatient to get off the bus. Several hours on a bus is not his idea of a good time, especially since Lizzie Doran sits behind them on the bus.

It's a tradition that Lizzie gets bus-sick on every class trip.

This trip is no exception.

Her mother now packs barf bags, plastic bags to put the barf bags in (no recycling of those bags), and a nonaerosol deodorizing spray.

Matthew thinks that the entire bus smells like a combination of Lizzie barf and pine forest.

Mr. Hudson calls out, "Mrs. Stanton. Look this way. Say cheese."

Mrs. Stanton does not say "cheese." In fact she does not look overjoyed at being filmed.

The clothes she has on are not her normal "teacher clothes." She is wearing jeans and a sweatshirt that says "Save the Whales."

Her eight-year-old daughter, Marie, is wearing jeans and a T-shirt that says "Save the Humans."

Mrs. Stanton explains. "When we get inside, everyone should stick together for a while. First I will register us and pick up our room assignment and schedule. Then we'll put our bags in the room, go see a film telling us about the institute, and have dinner. Remember, there will be no eating anywhere but in the designated areas."

Ryma's father raises his hand. "Is there a special area where adults can go to relax?"

Mrs. Stanton nods. "There is a leaders' lounge located in the employee lounge in the basement. Coffee and tea will be available. However, I do suggest that the chaperons see all of the exhibits and be available in case the students need them."

Mr. Browne says, "Absolutely. I just need a few minutes to relax."

Ryma calls out, "Translate that into, He just needs a few minutes to have a cigarette, which he shouldn't have anyway."

Several people on the bus hiss at the thought of cigarettes.

Mrs. Stanton shakes her head. "The museum has been designated a smoke-free environment."

There is applause.

Mr. Browne, however, does not look like a happy Camp-Iner.

Ryma looks up at her father and says softly, "Daddy, don't get upset, but you know that smoking's bad for you. I just worry."

Mr. Browne looks down at his only child and gives her a hug.

Mrs. Stanton continues. "You can probably smoke outside the building."

Mr. Browne shakes his head. "I'm going to try not to have a cigarette for the entire time we're here."

The entire bus cheers.

Mr. Browne looks down again at Ryma and says, "Maybe I should have one last cigarette on the street before we go in . . . since I haven't had one since we got on the bus. I didn't give my system any warning and . . ."

"Oh, Daddy, please," Ryma begs.

"Okay, I'll try," Mr. Browne promises.

"I've got that pledge on film." Mr. Hudson continues to point the camera at Mr. Browne. "How about if we have a shot of you handing your cigarettes to my wife for safekeeping?"

Mr. Hudson gets the picture of the cigarettes being passed to Mrs. Hudson, and one of the look of panic on Mr. Browne's face.

Mrs. Stanton says, "When we get settled inside, we will see the film telling about the museum and the rules and regulations. Then we'll be able to explore. Have fun . . . this is a wonderful place with lots of terrific things to do. Now, everyone out of the bus."

"Me first," Mr. Hudson yells. "I want to film everyone as they get off the bus."

"He filmed everyone as they got on the bus." Jil! sighs. "When will this ever end?"

People pile off the bus, carrying their plastic gear bags.

A group of the boys from Matthew's class gather by the door.

"Over here, Matthew," Joshua yells.

Matthew heads over to join them, and then he remembers . . . Jil!.

Standing in the middle, he looks back and forth, not sure what to do.

Again he wishes that there was a manual published with the rules and regulations for stuff like this.

"Come on, Matthew. What are you waiting for?" Joshua calls out.

Jil! waits for a minute to see what his decision is.

When it becomes obvious that no decision is on its way, she decides to make it easy for him—and for her too.

"Matthew Martin." She grins at him. "We are not Superglued to each other."

Matthew's feet finally become unglued from the sidewalk, and he rushes over to be with the other guys.

Zoe walks up to Jil! and says, "My mother's the real expert, with all the dating and marriages that she's been through. And she says that it's best to keep your eyes on them."

"Right now"—Jil! looks around—"it's The Franklin Institute that I want to keep my eyes on. Let's go inside."

Zoe heads off to where Tyler is waiting for her. "Don't say I didn't warn you."

Chapter 17

"Look at those little girls wearing feathers on their heads." Matthew points. "Maybe I should go over and tell them a couple of chicken jokes."

"They're from a Y group, Indian Princesses. They meet each week with their fathers. I know because my little sister is one and when I was little, I was an Indian guide and my dad went with me," Mark tells them. "It's nice that he does that, since he's allergic to feathers."

The downstairs is filling up as more and more people arrive. Some are dressed in Scout uniforms. One group is all wearing T-shirts that say "Edgar School Is Best." Almost everyone is wearing weekend clothes, except for one father, who is wearing a three-piece suit and carrying a briefcase. He goes up to one of the people in charge and says, "Has the group from Dover arrived yet?"

The woman handing out packets to group leaders checks her list and shakes her head.

"I just came from a business meeting in Philadelphia. Where is the men's room so that I can change?" He starts to loosen his tie. "Please let them know that Bill O'Brien is here already."

Matthew, who had been wondering if the man was planning on sleeping in the three-piece suit, says, "I'm never going to have a job where I have to get dressed up like that all day."

He remembers having to dress up for his uncle's wedding.

"What are you going to do?" Joshua starts to laugh. "Get a job as a model for a nudist catalog?"

Matthew punches his best friend on the arm. "I said that I didn't want to dress like that. . . . I didn't say I didn't want to dress."

"You could be a lifeguard . . . a garbage man . . . a cowboy . . . a basketball player." These are some of the suggestions that Matthew's friends make.

Basketball player is the suggestion that Matthew likes best, but he feels a little bad when he thinks about how he's not very tall.

He thinks about his family and how none of them

The Franklin Institute Science Museum

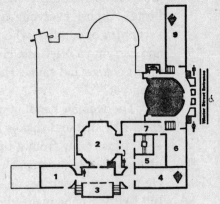

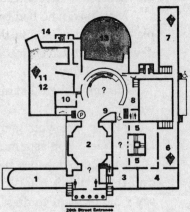

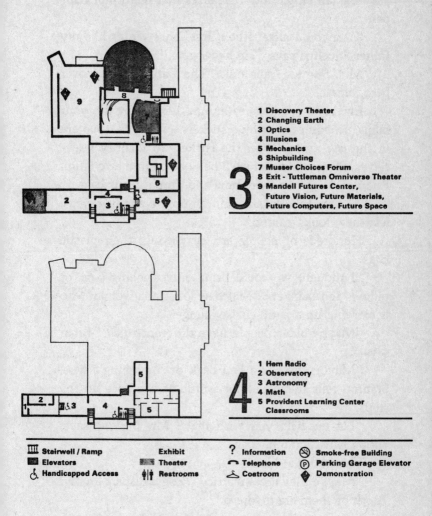

3

1 Discovery Theater
2 Changing Earth
3 Optics
4 Illusions
5 Mechanics
6 Shipbuilding
7 Musser Choices Forum
8 Exit - Tuttleman Omniverse Theater
9 Mandell Futures Center,
   Future Vision, Future Materials,
   Future Computers, Future Space

4

1 Ham Radio
2 Observatory
3 Astronomy
4 Math
5 Provident Learning Center
   Classrooms

IIII Stairwell / Ramp	Exhibit	? Information	Smoke-free Building
Elevators	Theater	Telephone	P Parking Garage Elevator
Handicapped Access	Restrooms	Coatroom	Demonstration

are very tall either and he realizes that might not happen.

"You could always be a free-lance writer like my father," Joshua says. "He never gets dressed up."

Mrs. Stanton calls out, "The Califon group over here, please."

Everyone congregates around her. "Here are your maps, schedules, and blue stickers. Notice that we are in the *blue* group. Wear the stickers to identify yourselves. Please note that we'll be sleeping in the Aviation Room. Let's go up there now and drop off our bags."

As they follow Mrs. Stanton up the winding steps, Matthew looks around.

Hundreds of people are carrying up their plastic bags.

"I thought we could bring only sleeping bags or pillows and blankets." Matthew looks at a woman who is carrying up a patio chaise lounge.

"Maybe older people have different rules," Brian says.

"Maybe she has a bad back or something," Mrs. Stanton tells them, puffing a little as she goes up the steps.

"Let me help you with that," Mr. Browne says, taking Mrs. Stanton's bag.

She smiles at him.

"Maybe they'll get married," Zoe whispers loudly. "Both of them are divorced."

"My parents are separated, not divorced yet." Ryma pokes Zoe on the arm, causing her to almost drop her bag.

Zoe grabs her bag more tightly and says, "Dream on. They don't get back together. I know that."

Patrick Ryan says nothing, but thinks about how bad it is between his parents.

Matthew thinks about how glad he is that his parents are happy with each other and wishes that Amanda would get a divorce from the Martin family. He thinks about the session with the family counselor when Amanda said her family couldn't understand her and he said that they just couldn't stand her.

"Aviation Room. Here we are." Mrs. Stanton points to the room. "Girls sleep in one place. Boys in another."

Airplanes hang from the ceiling. There are exhibit cases all over. In the middle of the room is a loft area, with more exhibits.

Lizzie points up to the loft. "Girls, let's sleep up there."

Matthew wonders if Lizzie has ever been loft-sick and decides not to sleep in the area below the loft, just in case.

"Okay. I just don't want to sleep under the plane in case it decides to fall down." Sarah bites her fingernail.

"It won't fall down, ditz-brain." Billy shakes his head.

Sarah continues to stare up at the plane.

"Come on!" Jil! yells. "Let's get the loft area before one of the other groups does."

"Okay," David Cohen teases.

"Girls only." Vanessa folds her arms. "You know

what Mrs. Stanton said: Boys in one place, girls in the other."

"Enough." Jil! rushes up the stairs. "If we don't get up there, someone else will get it."

She reaches the top of the stairs, throws her gear into the corner, and yells, "I claim this area for the Califon girls."

The boys decide to sleep by the exhibit directly across from where the girls are but far enough away so that if the girls decide to drop something on them, it won't reach.

Soon gear bags are stored. Dinner bags are all in hand. And everyone is ready.

"Forward, march." Mrs. Stanton pretends to act like a drill sergeant. "Let the good times roll."

Chapter 18

The Franklin Institute presents Camp-In

Evening Schedule

6:00 P.M.   ARRIVAL! Welcome to the program. Follow your dinner schedule. Visit exhibits.

7:00–7:30   PRE-WORKSHOP DEMONSTRATIONS
Papermaking—Communications, first floor
Static Show—Electricity, second floor

7:45   Start moving to Science Auditorium, first
               floor.

7:55–8:30   EUREKA! Insight and Invention

8:30–8:45   FIRST GROUP MEETING, Science Audi-
               torium

8:45–10:30   MUSEUM TIME
               Explore four floors of exhibit.
               Follow the museum map.

               SPECIALS TONIGHT
9:00–10:15   THE WONDERFUL WORLD OF WIND-
               UP
               Wind up a few friendly characters in this
               land of spring-powered toys. Bicycles—
               first floor

9:15–10:00   SNACKS
               Hungry? Come to Lunchbox for juice
               and crackers. No food beyond this point.

9:30–10:15   DISCO-MANIA
               Dance to your favorite songs in Express
               —first floor

10:15	Start moving to the planetarium—first floor.
10:30–11:05	PLANETARIUM SHOW—first floor, Fels Planetarium
11:05–11:15	SECOND GROUP MEETING—planetarium
11:15–11:45	CAMPSITES—Get ready for bed.
11:45	QUIET HOURS begin. Shhhhhhhhhhhh-hhhhhhhh!
12:00	LIGHTS OUT. Adults must accompany campers if they leave campsites. Nighty nite!!

"Awesome. This place is absolutely awesome." Matthew looks at the Shadow Freezer.

Joshua grins. "This may be even better than going through the heart."

The boys start to laugh when they think of how much fun it was going through the model of the heart, how they pretended to be corpuscles, how they hid inside and yelled "Phlegm" at some girls entering the lungs.

"You've got to admit that my personal best time of twenty-three seconds running through the heart was unbeatable," Joshua brags.

"I could have done better," Matthew defends himself, "if I hadn't gotten behind the lady who was yelling, 'Get me out of here. I'm claustrophobic.' Getting her out of there cost me a lot of time."

Joshua laughs at the memory. "She kept calling you a hero and saying that she practically had a heart attack in the heart."

Matthew keeps looking at the Shadow Freezer. "I wish those Indian Princesses and their feathers and their fathers would get out of there so we can go in."

Billy, Brian, and Pablo join them.

"How does that thing work?" Brian asks.

"You push the button and then pose in front of the screen until the lights flash. Then you step back and see your own shadow." Matthew looks at a father holding an Indian Princess by her ankles and then setting her down so that they can watch their shadows. "Awesome."

The boys move closer to the Shadow Freezer area and start making loud hints.

"Boy. I sure would like to try that."

"That looks like fun. I hope we get a chance soon."

"What time is it?"

"I bet you Indian Princesses haven't seen the heart yet. You're really going to like it. And don't forget about the Physics Room, where you can do balancing things with weights."

The Indian Princesses and their fathers finally move on, and the boys rush into the area.

All of them start grunting and doing karate moves.

"These shadows look awesome." Billy poses like he's a muscle man.

Matthew looks to his left and sees Mr. Hudson filming them.

"Pretty good, huh?" Matthew says, making hand-puppet motions.

Mrs. Stanton comes up to the Shadow Freezer. She asks, "Did you boys get to the Static Show?"

They shake their heads no.

"You missed something really terrific. The demonstrator made Vanessa's hair stand up on end by generating static."

"He should have demonstrated the electric chair on Vanessa." Matthew grins.

Mrs. Stanton ignores his statement. "They tried it with another girl, but she had too much mousse in her hair and it didn't work."

Mr. Browne joins them. He is biting a fingernail.

"How are you doing? Have you had a cigarette yet?" The boys want to know.

He shakes his head and smiles. "Not yet. Not since four o'clock. That makes it five hours, fifteen minutes, and thirty seconds since I've had one."

The boys cheer.

"How about letting someone else use this area?" Mrs. Stanton suggests, looking around at the group that is waiting.

The boys finally allow others to use it.

Mrs. Stanton says to them, "Did you like the Eureka Show? Wasn't it great the way they made it look as if they'd brought Benjamin Franklin back from the past to talk about his inventions and about his life and how things in science work?"

"I especially liked how Joshua got chosen from the audience to help build something on the earthquake machine and how his team won." Matthew grins and looks at his watch. "You know what else I like? It's snacktime."

"A truly educational experience for you," Mrs. Stanton teases.

"Snacktime. Great idea," Billy says. "We can get something to eat and then go watch the girls act doofy. They said that they were going to the disco, and that's right next to the snack place."

The boys rush down to the snack area.

Matthew has no idea that a very annoyed Jill is looking for him.

Chapter 19

Matthew is drinking his fifth container of apple juice and eating his sixth helping of cheese and crackers.

He is considering buying candy and soda with some of the money that his parents gave him to spend at the gift shop.

Two of the Camp-In staff members walk by. One is using a walkie-talkie. The other is holding the hand of a little boy who has gotten lost.

Matthew thinks about how great all the people

who work at Camp-In are, how a lot of them are only in high school and college, how he would like to work there someday.

"Jil! is looking for you," Cathy Atwood says as she heads to the vending machine.

Joshua crosses his arms and sticks his hands behind his back. Pantomiming a couple kissing, he says, "Oh, Jil! . . . Oh, Matthew . . . Oh, barf."

"You can't do anything without Jil!," Patrick taunts.

"Can too." Matthew sticks another cracker in his mouth.

"Can not," Joshua tells him. "Every time I'm looking for you, you're with Jil!."

"Not true." Matthew defends himself, thinking about how he spends a lot of time with the guys in his class.

Joshua, seeing how much Matthew is blushing, continues. "You like Jil! even more than your computer . . . even more than Nintendo . . . even more than brownies and ice cream."

Matthew is more used to teasing someone than being teased and isn't sure of what to say.

"Jil! is looking for you." Her younger brother, Jonathan, comes running up to tell him. "Am I glad I'm not you right now."

"Jil! is looking for you," Patrick mimics, using a whiny voice.

The boys start to laugh, all except Matthew.

Mr. Hudson comes up, points the camera at everyone, and says, "Smile. Hold up those juice cartons."

Everyone but Matthew holds up the juice carton. Everyone but Matthew smiles.

Matthew gets up from the table. "Bye."

"Running away?" Joshua looks at him. "Or are you rushing to her because she commands?"

Matthew walks out the door.

"Jil! wants to see you," Zoe and Tyler call out.

Matthew is getting very annoyed. "No fooling. I never would have guessed."

He heads into the disco room.

It's very dark.

Strobe lights are going.

There are a lot of people dancing. Girls and boys together. Girls with girls. Girls dancing alone. Boys dancing alone. Boys slamming into each other and throwing rubber lavalike rocks at each other.

Matthew watches as two grown-ups try to do the latest dance.

He is glad that they are not his parents and feels sorry for the kid whose parents they are.

"Jil!'s looking for you." Lisa slows down her dancing long enough to call out to him.

"Duh," Matthew mutters.

By the water fountain he finds Jil!.

"I've been looking for you," she tells him.

Matthew, by this time, is sick of hearing about how she's looking for him. "Well, you found me. What do you want?"

She shrugs. "I just thought we could dance together. I haven't seen you all night."

Several of their classmates come over and stand nearby so that they can hear the conversation.

Patrick says nothing but flaps his arms.

Joshua grins.

Softly Jil! says, "Tyler dances with Zoe. You could dance with me."

Everyone waits for Matthew's answer.

Instead of speaking, he grabs Jil! by the hand and takes her out to where people are dancing.

Looking over at the guys who have been teasing him, he starts to dance the way he thinks a chicken would.

Jil! looks at him and says, "Matthew. Stop that. You're so embarrassing."

Matthew looks at her and then looks at the guys and then looks back at Jil! and clucks.

She puts her hands on her hips. "Matthew Martin. How can you do this to me? I hate you. I don't ever want to speak to you again."

She turns around and walks away.

Just as Matthew decides to follow after her and explain that he was just joking around because he doesn't know how to dance and because all of his friends are teasing him, he feels someone punch him on the shoulder.

It's Joshua. "Way to go! You really showed her."

Patrick raises his hand and gives him a high five.

The lights come on in the disco, and one of the leaders announces that it is time to go to the planetarium.

As everyone heads to the second floor, Matthew looks for Jil!.

Somehow he knows that they're not going to be sitting together for this show.

And he realizes that he's not very happy about it.

Chapter 20

"Lights out. Everyone to sleep." The person from Camp-In switches off the lights in the Aviation Room.

Matthew gets hit on the head with a pillow.

It's Joshua.

Matthew hits Joshua back. "Leave me alone, duh-brain."

Joshua hits him again with a pillow and then hits Brian, who hits Tyler and Billy.

Soon all the boys from Califon are hitting each other with pillows.

Soon kids from other groups are hitting the kids from their own groups with pillows.

There's laughing and name-calling.

The lights go on and a man says, "That's enough. I want you all to go to sleep. We have a busy day tomorrow."

The lights go out again.

It's quiet.

Someone starts giggling in a corner and soon that whole corner is giggling.

One of the girls in that group has the kind of laugh that makes everyone start laughing.

The lights go on again. "It's after midnight. I want you all to go to sleep."

It quiets down and the lights go off again.

Some people actually manage to go to sleep.

One group is in a corner whispering the grossest jokes they know. An Indian Princess's father starts snoring—very loudly.

Matthew wonders what it's like for the people who are sleeping in the room with the heart, whether the heart keeps pumping all night.

He also wonders whether Jil! is ever going to talk to him, ever again.

She didn't stop when he tried to talk to her after the planetarium show.

She turned away when he tried to talk to her when they all got back into the Aviation Room, when he invited her to go sit up in the cockpit of the plane.

Matthew Martin is angry. He's angry at Jil! for ignoring him. He's angry at his friends for teasing him.

He's angry at himself for acting so dumb when he doesn't know what to do.

Matthew listens to the snores of the Indian Princess's father and wonders about why everything is getting so complicated.

He listens to the laughter of the corner group and then thinks about how he isn't even a teenager yet, how he's only eleven, how everything around him is changing.

He wonders whether Califon School is part of an ecosystem of its own and whether what happens to each of the kids in his class affects the other kids.

He thinks maybe that's true because he knows that Joshua has been acting different since Jil! and Matthew started to go out.

Thinking about the ecosystem makes Matthew think about food chains in nature. Thinking about food chains makes him think about McDonald's and makes him wish he'd eaten more at snacktime.

He pokes Joshua on his side and whispers, "Got anything to eat?"

Joshua rolls over and pulls something out of his sleeping bag. "I've got some astronaut ice cream."

"Where did you get it?" Matthew asks, taking a chunk of the freeze-dried ice cream.

"The gift shop," Joshua says, eating some of it. "Good, huh? Weird but good."

All around the room Matthew can hear sounds.

Snoring.

One little girl is talking to the huge stuffed bear she brought in her gear bag.

Giggling.

Matthew can hear giggling from the loft area.

He wonders if all the girls are laughing at him.

He's always liked to make everyone laugh, but not like this.

He wonders if Jil! is even thinking about him.

Matthew pokes Billy. "Lend me the glow stick."

Billy passes over the fluorescent light stick he bought at the gift shop.

Matthew uses it to look at his watch.

1:38 A.M.

And all is not well.

Chapter 21

A voice comes over the intercom. "Attention K mart shoppers. There's a special on dog food in Aisle 3. Limited supply available."

Matthew sits up.

Someone has captured the intercom.

Someone else captures the kid who has captured the intercom and all is quiet again.

Looking at his watch, Matthew sees that it is 6:00 A.M.

He also sees that people are starting to wake up.

There are still people who are sound asleep.

The snoring Indian Princess's father continues to snore. He also grunts.

Matthew looks at his friends.

Pablo has totally covered himself with his sleeping bag.

Joshua has fallen asleep with his head on what was left of the astronaut ice cream, and there are freeze-dried ice cream crumbs on his face and in his hair.

Billy is sound asleep with his thumb in his mouth.

Matthew plans to remember that if Billy ever teases him about Jil!

Matthew looks up to see Mr. Hudson filming everyone start to wake up.

He sees that Jil! is walking across the room with her toothbrush in her hand.

Matthew jumps up.

Stepping over sleeping and waking-up bodies, he follows her out the door.

"Wait up," he calls out.

"Shhh." Someone punches him on the ankle.

Hopping out of the door, he runs into Jil!, who stands there glaring at him. "What do you want?"

"I want to talk to you," he says.

"Shhhh" is the sound from just inside the door.

"Please." Matthew looks her in the eyes. "I really want to talk to you."

"I don't want to talk to you." Jil! stamps her foot.

"And I don't want to hear either of you talking to each other at this hour." An adult voice can be heard from just inside the door.

"Let's go over there." Matthew points to a spot down the hallway.

Jil! looks at Matthew and shrugs.

He gets down on bended knee and begs. "Oh, please."

"Quiet down, out there." The adult voice sounds more annoyed.

"Okay, Matthew Martin," Jil! whispers. "But just for a minute so that I can tell you what I think of you."

Matthew and Jil! go stand in a corner.

"You totally embarrassed me. All I wanted to do was spend some time with you and you acted like a real goof . . . showing off in front of everyone." Jil! bites her lip to keep from crying.

Matthew nods. "I know. But I was beginning to feel like I was number one of the Ten Most Wanted . . . like finding me was an unsolved mystery for everyone and their brother—actually everyone and your brother."

Jil! nods back. "I know. All the girls were teasing me and making me feel like we should be together even though I was having fun being with them. Zoe kept telling me that you had probably found someone from another school that you liked better."

"That's dumb." Matthew makes a face. "I've only just started liking girls. And you're the one that I like, so why should I like someone else? Liking you is confusing enough."

Jil! grins. "I know what you mean. How come I can't just like you and you like me without everyone else treating us like we're a television show or something?"

"Like a Federation of Wrestling show?" Matthew starts to laugh. "Or a cartoon show?"

Mr. Hudson comes up to them and starts filming them.

Jil! looks at her father. "Daddy. Would you please stop that? When are you going to realize that I'm growing up and I have my own life? When are you going to allow me some of the privacy that I need to become my own person?"

Mr. Hudson puts down his camera and looks at his daughter, not sure of what to say.

"Oops." He walks away to think about what his daughter has just told him.

"Wow." Matthew looks at Jil!. "I can't believe that you said that."

"I saw this show on *Oprah* that talked about parents and kids. I decided to try it out." Jil! is feeling much better.

"Did *Oprah* have a show on the relationships of eleven-year-olds? If not, I think we should write to her and offer to be on the show." Matthew laughs.

Jil! laughs too.

"Look. I'm sorry that I acted like a goofus," Matthew tells her.

"Me too." Jil! nods.

"So we can just be our age and like each other without it getting too mushy?" Matthew feels much better.

"Agreed." Jil! reaches out to shake his hand.

131

Matthew shakes her hand and then starts to wrestle with it.

They both start to laugh.

Matthew leans over and gives her a little kiss on her cheek.

They stand there looking at each other for a minute.

"Maybe being a teenager won't be so bad," Matthew says.

"Yeah," Jil! agrees.

"Yeah. I can get my driver's license then." Matthew grins.

"Doofus." Jil! gives his arm a little punch.

And so Day 2 at The Franklin Institute begins.

Chapter 22

MORNING SCHEDULE

6:30 A.M.   WAKE UP! Good morning.
                   CLEAN AREA. Pick up gear. Follow
                   directions by staff to storage area.

6:45–7:30   BREAKFAST. Go to Lunchbox Area.

7:45–11:30   VISIT THE FUTURES CENTER.
                   See the film at the Omniverse The-
                   ater.

Visit exhibits.
Attend workshops.

11:30   DEPARTURE BEGINS.
               All groups head toward the Science
               Auditorium to pick up gear. Use
               Winter Street doors to exit. Thanks
               for coming. See you next year.

"Breakfast." Matthew races toward the eating area. "It's my favorite meal of the morning and I don't want to miss it."

"It's the only meal of the morning," Jil! reminds him as she races alongside him. "Matthew, stop . . . look."

Pointing to a green machine, Jil! says, "It's called a medal maker. You know, one of those old things that stamps whatever you want to say on a round medal."

"Breakfast." Matthew holds his stomach.

"Please," Jil! begs. "I'll give you my doughnut if you wait just a few minutes."

Matthew thinks about two doughnuts instead of one. Not only will he have more to eat but first he can hold one up to each eye, look through the hole, and yell "Glasses." Then when he has only a little bit of doughnut left around the holes, he can hold them up to his eyes and yell "Contact lenses."

"It's a deal." He grins at Jil!, who is wearing an extra-large Futures Center T-shirt as a dress. On her feet are pink sparkly socks and sandals.

She grins back at Matthew, who has on a Camp-In T-shirt. "It'll be the souvenir of our visit."

"Oh, okay," Matthew says. "What are we going to write on it?"

Jil! blushes. "I kind of thought we could write our names on it and the date. The medal already says The Franklin Institute." Jil! takes a quarter out of her belt pouch.

Digging into his pocket, Matthew says, "I'll pay for it."

The quarter goes into the machine, and Matthew and Jil! imprint their names on the medal. Jil! adds the date.

Picking up the finished medal, Jil! says, "This is great. I can put it on a chain and wear it as a necklace."

"Does this mean we're engaged?" Matthew thinks about how the guys are going to react to the medal.

"No. It doesn't mean we're engaged." Jil! looks at him. "If you don't want me to wear it, I won't. In fact if you want me to, I can just throw it away and forget about it."

Matthew can tell that Jil! will not just throw it away and forget about it.

He realizes that he probably is not handling this situation as well as he could, so he says, "Don't get angry. I don't want us to be engaged and I don't want you to be enraged. And I think it will be nice for you to wear the medal. Now can we go to breakfast, please . . . ?"

Jil! says, "Don't you want a medal, too, as a souvenir?"

Shaking his head, Matthew says, "No. Actually there's something in the store that I want as a souvenir. It's a basketball with a map of the world on it."

How romantic, Jil! thinks.

"Breakfast." Matthew starts to run. "We better get going."

Racing down the hall, Jil! holds the medal tightly in her hand.

Matthew thinks about how hungry he is.

"Slow down," one of the teachers from another school calls out to them.

Matthew thinks about how "Slow down" must be on a list of phrases that a teacher has to learn before getting in front of a class.

Arriving at the cafeteria, they get their breakfasts and sit down with some of the Califon group.

Jil! hands Matthew her chocolate-covered doughnut.

Matthew holds up both doughnuts and yells "Glasses."

He then slurps down his juice.

Mrs. Stanton hands him a spoon. "I brought these from home. They asked that we all bring our own spoons that we can take home again so that they didn't have to use plastic utensils."

Matthew quickly eats around the doughnuts, leaving a little cake around the holes.

Continuing, Mrs. Stanton picks up her coffee cup, which says "#1 Teacher." "And I like the fact that they are using reusable and recyclable products whenever possible . . . and that they asked adults to bring their own mugs."

"Why don't we have Mr. Hudson take a picture of you and your cup and then it would be a mug shot?" Mr. Browne smiles and sits down next to Mrs. Stanton.

Zoe looks at them and wonders if her teacher and Ryma's father ever do date and marry, will they let her be a bridesmaid. She already has several dresses from her parents' weddings.

"How is it going? Be honest. Have you really not smoked yet?" Matthew asks.

Looking at his watch, Mr. Browne says, "Fourteen hours, fifty-five minutes, and sixteen seconds. And how could I smoke? Every time I turned around, one of you was following me."

"We took shifts. I organized it."

"Thank you . . . I think." Mr. Browne smiles. "It would have been nice, though, to have had a little more privacy in the bathroom."

"I really did have to go," Billy says, turning red.

"We had to check on you," Vanessa tells Mr. Browne. "People going through withdrawal can*not* be trusted. I know . . . my mother gave up smoking seven times before she really quit."

Matthew looks at Vanessa and thinks about how nice it was that she organized everything to help Mr. Browne.

Then he remembers all the anti-Matthew things she organizes and stops thinking positively about her.

Billy Kellerman is asleep with his head on the table.

Lisa Levine is pulling strands of his hair through Cheerios and then putting a little knot at the end.

"Disney World and Paris would have been wonderful." Matthew turns to Mrs. Stanton, who has just handed her doughnut to Mr. Browne. "But The Franklin Institute is great."

Mrs. Stanton looks at everyone at the table. "Do you want to know the best thing?"

Everyone does.

"The best thing is that our visit isn't over, that we get to see the Futures Center this morning."

Matthew gets up with his tray. "I'm ready for the twenty-first century. I hope it's ready for me."

Jil! gets up also. "I'm ready too."

"I thought you were going to go to the Futures Center with us." Joshua looks at Matthew.

Patrick flaps his arms. "Cluck. Cluck."

Matthew looks at him. "Wrong animal, Patrick. You ought to pretend to be the animal you're acting like, actually the part of the animal you're acting like. Say 'Neigh' and turn around."

Patrick stops clucking.

Matthew says, "Jil! and I are going to the Futures Center. Let's all go together."

Joshua looks uncertain.

"Come on. I hear that there is a Jamming Room."

"I thought they didn't allow food in the museum part." Joshua looks confused.

Ryma giggles. "The Jamming Room has a drum pad, marimba, and keyboard. It's to make music."

"I knew that." Joshua pretends that he really did know that.

Everyone gets up and heads off to the Center, everyone, including Billy Kellerman, who has awakened and doesn't know that he has turned into a Cheeriohead.

Matthew makes a fast stop at the gift shop and picks up his globe basketball.

As everyone enters the door below a neon sign, Matthew walks backward and says, "Everyone do this with me . . . and it'll be *Back to the Future.*"

"Let's not and say we did," Vanessa mumbles.

They all walk in . . . backward or forward.

And are in the middle of the twenty-first century.

Chapter 23

"Amazing. This place is absolutely amazing," Jil!
says as everyone enters the Future Vision gateway exhibit.

Mrs. Stanton looks at a map. "There are eight main
exhibits: Future Vision, Future Materials, Future Computers, Future Space, Future Energy, Future Earth, Fu-
ture Health, and The Future and You."

Everyone thinks about which place to go to first.

Mrs. Stanton continues. "Don't forget, I have the
Unisys card and if you want any information from any

of the computers, find me and we'll use the card and activate the printer."

She holds up the bar-coded card, which gives her access to a computer information network in the museum, one that links the Futures and Science centers and can help plan specialized tours of the institute and get information. It will also help her get information and lessons to use later with the class.

"Lucky," Matthew says. "How come only leaders get those cards?"

"Because the machines would overload," Mrs. Stanton informs him. "When you come back on your own, you'll be able to get one of these cards. Listen, there's so much to do and not a lot of time. You'd all better get going."

Everyone rushes off to the exhibits.

As Jil! and Matthew stand by the large model of the earth, her father comes up to them.

He is still holding the camera.

Matthew wonders if the camera has become permanently attached to Mr. Hudson's body.

Mr. Hudson says, "I would really like to take a picture of you in front of the globe."

Jil! and Matthew look at each other.

"Oh, okay," they both say.

Mr. Hudson aims the camera. "I want you both to stand in front of the globe. Matthew, I want you to hold your basketball in front of you."

Matthew bounces the ball.

The teacher who had earlier told them to stop running walks by and tells him to stop bouncing the ball.

Matthew twirls the ball on his finger.

Mr. Hudson says, "I want you both to smile."

Jil! says, "I want you to take this film so that we can see the museum before we have to go."

"Get ready," Mr. Hudson calls out.

Matthew continues to twirl the basketball.

Jil! holds up the medal.

Mr. Hudson films.

"It's a wrap," Mr. Hudson yells.

"My father really wanted to be a director." Jil! turns to Matthew.

Mr. Hudson walks away, and Jil! and Matthew continue to explore the Futures Center.

Chapter 24

"It's not fair." Matthew looks around at the Future Earth Exhibit.

"What's not?" Jil! asks.

"I work out my problems. You're not mad at me. My other friends aren't mad at me, except for maybe Amanda and Vanessa, who hate every one of my guts and I don't care about them." Matthew points to the twelve-foot model of the earth. "Look at that. It shows what's happening to the planet . . . acid rain . . . the greenhouse effect . . . the ozone layer . . . It's so depressing."

Jil! points to another area. "But look. There's also an exhibit about how we can help."

They walk over to it.

"There's so much to do and it isn't even my fault. I don't want to think about it, but I have to think about it." Matthew walks over to an exhibit and starts to smile. "Jil!. Look. It's a miniature rain forest ecosystem . . . system . . . system. . . ."

As they walk around the exhibits, Jil! says, "I've been doing a lot of thinking. None of us can do all the things that will save the planet but each of us can do some of them and all of that will add up and be better than nothing."

"Boy, you guys are very serious," Billy Kellerman says. "Lighten up a little."

"And you are being very cereal." Matthew looks at Billy and laughs.

"I don't get it." Billy looks puzzled.

Matthew points to one of the staff members who is wearing a shirt with EXPLAINER written on the back. "Ask him."

Billy shakes his head. Several of the Cheerios fall off.

"Dandruff alert!" Patrick yells.

Lizzie tries to look innocent.

Billy heads off to the boys' room, vowing never to trust his classmates again.

Matthew calls out to him. "Some people get their hair corn-rowed. You got yours Oat Bran-rowed."

Matthew has a great time as the group goes through the rest of the exhibits.

There is so much to do.

He finds out how much he weighs on Earth . . . Also on Mars, Jupiter, and Venus.

He calls Mrs. Stanton over.

She refuses to weigh herself.

He and Jil! stand in front of a machine that shows their images on the wall and then lets them make patterns and colors on the images.

Matthew ends up red and striped.

Jil! becomes purple and polka-dotted.

Everyone in the class runs around trying out all the machines.

Matthew stands in front of a robot sensor and keeps jumping up and down while the sensor tries to measure his height.

The machine keeps telling him to stop squirming, to stay in one place. Finally Matthew stands still and the machine calls out his exact height.

An Indian Princess's father comes over and is measured at five feet eleven inches. He steps back and then returns, putting his arms above his head. The machine then tells him that he is six feet ten inches and must be eating his Wheaties.

Next comes the Space Tools Exhibit.

Jil! is chosen to demonstrate some of the wearable equipment and looks like a human robot.

Then a group of people look at the recyclable art.

A huge sculpture has been made out of all kinds of garbage thrown together.

"That looks like my room." Joshua laughs.

The tour continues.

Mr. Hudson stands by the large picture of the astronaut uniform. In the middle of the helmet is a hole in which people put their heads and pretend to be astronauts.

As Califon students come by, Mr. Hudson has each of them go behind the photo and use the steps to get up high enough to insert their heads in the hole.

"This will be filed under 'Califon Sixth-graders— Space Cadets.'" Mr. Hudson takes a picture of Billy Kellerman, who has removed most of the Cheerios from his head.

Jil!'s mother tries out a machine that shows what she will look like in twenty years.

"Yuck," is her reaction.

"Look, Matthew." Jil! points out several quotations on the wall. "Look at that one from President John F. Kennedy."

"MAN IS STILL THE MOST EXTRAORDINARY COMPUTER OF ALL."

Matthew, who loves computers, smiles.

He likes being called a computer.

He also knows that he likes being a person.

Computers can't eat junk food.

Computers can't have friends.

Mrs. Stanton stands next to her students. "Look at the quote from Woody Allen."

"IT'S CLEAR THE FUTURE HOLDS GREAT OPPORTU-
NITIES.

IT ALSO HOLDS PITFALLS. THE TRICK WILL BE TO
AVOID THE PITFALLS, SEIZE THE OPPORTUNITIES, AND
GET BACK HOME BY SIX O'CLOCK."

Looking at the Woody Allen quote on the wall,
Mrs. Stanton says, "That reminds me. We have to get
ready to leave. Our time at The Franklin Institute is
over. It's almost eleven thirty."

"Ratsafrats," Jil! says. "I feel like Cinderella."

Everyone heads down to the area where the bags
are stored.

Then everyone has to wait until Tyler and Zoe are
located.

Outside the museum Mr. Hudson takes videos of
the group.

Many of them are wearing the clothes that they
have slept in.

Some have their new T-shirts on.

A few of them are having trouble staying awake.

Mrs. Stanton and Mr. Browne stand next to each
other, smiling.

Mrs. Stanton's daughter, Marie, and Ryma Browne
look at each other trying to figure out what it would be
like if they became sisters.

Matthew and Jil! stand next to each other.

He's making devil's horns behind her head.

"On the bus, everyone." Mrs. Stanton calls out.

People rush onto the bus, trying to get a seat that is
not near Lizzie Duran.

Everyone gets on.

Matthew and Jil! sit together.

Joshua, sitting behind them, drops some astronaut ice cream on Matthew's head.

When Matthew turns around, he sees Ryma sitting next to Joshua.

Joshua flashes his best friend a look that says, "You're dead meat if you open your mouth."

Matthew hums a few bars of "Here Comes the Bride" and sits down again.

Mrs. Stanton counts heads.

The driver starts the bus.

It's back to Califon . . . before six o'clock.

Matthew thinks about how much has happened in sixth grade and wonders what it's going to be like when school is over.

Jil! raps him on his head with her knuckles. "Earth to Matthew. Do you read me? Please make contact."

Matthew pretends to pick up a phone. "Matthew to earth. I read you loud and clear."

Matthew feels as if he is on a spaceship, Spaceship Earth.

And he can't wait to see where it takes him next.